SOCCER SISTERS

Li

Out of Bounds

"This is exactly the kind of book I wish
I'd had the chance to read as a girl"
- Brandi Chastain

Andrea Montalbano

A Letter from Brandi Chastain

Hi Everyone!

Soccer is one of the greatest sports in the world. I should know, I've been playing it basically all my life. I was always that kid down at the schoolyard kicking the ball against the wall or juggling in my front yard. I was willing to do whatever it took to get better.

Plus, it was fun and I loved it.

I still do. There is no better sport to teach you how to be a team player, make friends, and keep you healthy and strong.

Playing soccer provided me with so many amazing

opportunities! From playing in two World Cups to having the privilege of representing my country in the Olympics.

One thing I didn't have when I was growing up were books about soccer players. I wish I had had Soccer Sisters to read when I was a kid!

Lily, Vee, Tabitha, and all the Bombers have so many adventures and exciting games on the field. Reading Soccer Sisters takes me right in the middle of the action – my favorite place – and I know you will love it too.

I hope you enjoy Soccer Sisters as much as I do and remember, you can become a true champion if you always work to achieve your personal best.

Keep reading and kicking!

Brandi Chastain

Praise for *Soccer Sisters*

Napa County Reads 2012 Official Selection

"The *Soccer Sisters* series isn't just about soccer. It's about friendships, family and the awesome thrill that comes from winning. It's also fun, which is the best reason in the world to read it." —Carl Hiaasen

Praise for *Breakaway* by Andrea Montalbano

"A winning book by a talented newcomer." —Mike Lupica

"Montalbano's love of the game is evident in the detailed, technical description of each play. Her description of youth sports tackles fanatical fans, overbearing parents, and jealous peers." —Kirkus Reviews

"It's an ideal pick for readers more interested in scoring goals than boyfriends." —Publishers Weekly

Soccer Sisters

Book 1

Lily Out of Bounds

Andrea Montalbano

In This Together Media

Published July 2012 in the United States of America
by In This Together Media, New York

ISBN-13: 978-0-9858956-1-7

BISAC: 1. Soccer (Sports & Recreation) — Juvenile
Fiction. 2. Girls and Women — Juvenile Fiction.

Cover Design and Photo: Evan Rich
evanrphotography.com

Soccer Sisters Team Code

1. Team first.
2. Don't be a poor sport or loser.
3. Play with each other and don't take the fun out of it.
4. Never put someone down if they make a mistake.
5. Practice makes perfect.
6. Never give up on the field or on one another.
7. Leave it on the field.
8. Always do the right thing.
9. Bring snacks on assigned days.
10. Beat the boys at recess soccer.

Go Bombers???

Chapter 1.

It's not always easy to know right from wrong, especially when you're a kid.

Sure, parents try to help. *Look both ways,* they remind you. *Don't wallop your brother. No kicking the ball in the house. Finish your homework.* And that old favorite: *Get to bed.*

Lily James had heard it all in her thirteen years. She listened as best she could. She mostly left her little brother, Billy, alone. If she hit him, she did it when no one could see, which she thought should count for something. She hadn't been taken out by a car, she had clean-ish teeth, and, in general, she slept at night.

The "no kicking the ball in the house" thing was tougher.

For Lily, kicking a soccer ball was as vital as taking a breath. Did her parents really expect her not to breathe in the house?

Lily's mom and dad did do their best to support her obsession with soccer, because they both had their own passions. For her father, Liam, it was food and cooking. He owned a small restaurant in their hometown of Brookville called "Katerina's," where he spent hours concocting special recipes. Then there was Lily's mother. She loved bugs. Seriously. Toni James was the world's foremost expert on butterflies and other insects, which Lily thought made her both weird and cool.

As usual, both Lily's parents were too busy to make it to today's game, the kick off to the Long Island Memorial Day Cup, one of the biggest tournaments in the Northeast. The teams and fans were gathering on the fields, and Lily breathed in the scene. Every one of her senses absorbed the pre-game bustle. She inhaled the smell of the young summer grass and listened to the murmur of coaches and players huddled together whispering about line-ups and strategy. She ached for the feeling of freedom and for the joy of dribbling a ball down the field. She adored running strong and playing tough.

Lily loved everything about soccer.

Straightening out her blue and yellow Brookville Bombers uniform, Lily sized up their opponents, the Ocean View Wildcats, who were stretching in a circle on the other side of the field. Lily knew they were the tournament's defending champions. She and the

Bombers were facing a tough game. Lily checked her laces and grabbed her neon green ball.

"Ready?" she asked her best friend, Vee Merino, who was plopped on the ground beside her.

"You know I'm not." The answer came quickly.

Lily sighed and watched with amused eyes as her BFF went through her sacred pre-game checklist. Lily knew it by heart. First, Vee double-knotted her laces. Then she meticulously tucked the tips into the sides of her shoes (Vee couldn't stand it when her laces flopped around during a game). Next, she fiddled with her shin guards, refolded her tube socks, and adjusted her headband. Several times.

"Ready now?" Lily asked, after the third headband adjustment.

"One last thing," Vee answered, checking her cleats for dirt. "Okay, ready."

"Finally!" Lily laughed, pulling Vee to her feet and dribbling quickly onto the field, making sharp moves to the left and right. Vee was beside her in a second. Lily laid off a pass to the right without even looking. Vee collected the ball and delivered it right back to Lily's foot. Neither girl ever broke stride.

That's how it was between Lily and Vee. They had known each other since they were babies, because Vee's father was the manager of Katerina's. Lily and Vee had been together on the Bombers for the last three years, but they had been kicking the ball around behind the restaurant for as long as either could remember. Vee lived in a neighboring town and went to a different school, but that hardly mattered.

Because Lily and Vee were sisters.

Not the kind of sister your mom and dad bring home from the hospital, but the kind of sister you choose.

The kind who picks you up and wipes you off when you fall face-first in the mud.

The kind who shares your passions through sunshine or rain, win or lose.

The kind who always has your back, no matter what.

Lily and Vee were connected in a way that had nothing to do with DNA, but everything to do with TEAM.

Lily and Vee were Soccer Sisters.

Physically, the two girls could not have looked more different. Lily was tall and Vee was tiny. Lily was fair with Irish freckles and bright eyes that were a mix of green, blue and yellow. Vee was from Mexico. Her skin was like cocoa, her hair was so black that in some lights it looked blue, and her big brown eyes were steady and warm. They weren't technically related, but soccer made them family.

The two girls moved in tandem toward the rest of the Bombers, who were taking shots on goal.

"So what do you know about this guest player?" Vee asked Lily as they waited to take their turns.

"Not much," Lily said, pushing the ball to her right and firing a shot toward the goal. As usual, both girls shared the same giddy pre-game anticipation, and today their excitement was doubled. They were expecting a new girl to join their team as a guest for the tournament.

"What position does she play?" Vee asked, gathering the ball back from the goalie.

"All I know is she's a mid-fielder, she's from here on Long Island, and she's really late," Lily said. She scanned the field for an unfamiliar face, but just saw her regular squad warming up. Beth was in goal, Olivia was trying to do some juggling, and the rest of the girls were starting a game of keep-away. The only person missing was Tabitha, who was away on a cruise with her family.

"What kind of player comes late to a tournament?" Vee asked in an annoyed voice. "The game's about to start."

"That's a good question," Lily said, looking around. "I guess we'll find out."

"Bombers! Bring it in!"

It was their coach, Chris Moore. He held up his clipboard with the line-up. Chris ran them through their positions and told them the guest player, a girl named Colby, was running a few minutes late. There was a little chatter among the Bombers, but seconds later, the referee blew his whistle and Lily and her team were swept away by the magic of the game.

The Wildcats lived up to their reputation. Before they knew it, the Bombers were losing 2-1. Today was one of those days when nothing was going their way. The ball wouldn't go in no matter how many shots they took. It was like there was an invisible screen in front of the goal. The ball hit the side posts and bounced into the goalie's hands. It sailed over the crossbar from impossible angles.

Bounce, bounce, bounce. Everywhere but into the back of the net.

Lily was keeping her cool, but she and the rest of her team were frustrated. They knew the clock was ticking.

"Lily! I'm open!" a girl screamed. "Lily! Give me the ball!"

It took a second for Lily James to register that the girl was calling to her. Everyone on the Bombers called her LJ.

She passed the ball quickly, but her two-second delay was too much. Her pass was intercepted by a blur in orange, and the ball went out of bounds.

"My bad, Colby," Lily called, apologizing for the bad pass. She ran over to take the throw. Colby jogged over to her.

"Lily, I'm going to fake a run down the line but then go into the middle. You get me the ball, okay?"

Lily nodded, a little hesitant. So this was her new teammate. She stared at Colby's face.

"Okay?" Colby asked again.

"Got it," Lily nodded, surer this time.

The guest player had arrived all right, along with weird excuses about getting lost. Her name was Colby Wrangle. She had short, spiky dark hair that flopped like a bird's wing when she ran. She wore a tattered black headband to keep the hair out of her eyes, which Lily thought made her look ultra-fierce. On one side of her head, her hair was cut super short and had a stripe dyed scarlet. To top it off, she had a tattoo on her lower arm that said "Glory," and she wore black stuff under her eyes like a football player.

No one said "no" to Colby Wrangle, Lily could tell.

Colby ran straight at Lily, and Lily faked the throw. The orange defender got in front of Colby, who made a quick turn and ran into the middle of the field. Lily quickly lifted the ball over her head and launched it as hard as she could. It floated over the confused defender's head. Colby brought the ball down and took off toward the goal.

Colby played with supreme confidence, Lily thought, tracking her downfield. She'd been unsure about having anyone new on the roster for such an important tournament, but with Tabitha away, they needed another player. Now Lily was psyched Colby was on their side. She certainly wouldn't want to have to play against her. Colby had already scored the Bomber's one goal of the morning off a direct kick. Lily didn't get a good view of the foul, but she sure saw that Colby had no problem finally getting the Bombers a goal.

Vee made a run down the line. Lily smiled. Vee was always tough, fast and brave.

"Colby!" Vee called, darting quickly across the grass.

Colby sent a beautiful lofting pass over the defense. Vee handled the high ball easily, bringing it down to her foot without losing speed. She took off toward the corner flags. Lily knew she was going to go for a cross.

An orange defender ran out to meet Vee. She was about twice Vee's size. Vee waited for the girl to get close, then pulled back her left foot like she was going for the cross. The fake worked. The Wildcat lunged to block the ball. Vee deftly dribbled around her and this time she really did launch a cross. It was perfect, floating high above the defenders with enough backspin that Lily knew it would come down in front of the goal.

Lily moved forward, tracking the ball and timing her jump.

Keeping her eyes glued on the ball, Lily launched herself into the air. A defender jumped with her, but Lily moved higher. The ball arrived; Lily flicked her head to the side. She felt the ball connect with the side of her head and heard the satisfying thump that sent it soaring toward the upper corner.

As she fell to the ground, she waited for the cheers to come. There was no way that ball hadn't gone in. She hit the grass with a thud, but heard only a whistle and the referee's call.

"Corner kick!"

Corner kick? How could that be?

"What happened?" Lily stammered.

"Goalie tipped it out of bounds." Colby was shaking her head. "Unbelievable."

Lily sprinted over to take the kick. She raised her hand to signal her teammates that she was ready. Colby, Vee and Olivia all put their hands up in reply.

Chris had moved the whole team into offense. It was now or never. Lily drove the ball as hard as she could towards the goal. This wasn't a long, loopy pass, but a hard-driven knuckler. There were so many girls crowded in front of the goal it was hard to see what was happening. First, the ball careened into the mix and bounced off the thigh of a defender. Olivia ran forward and tried to tap it in. The ball ricocheted off another Wildcat. It was like soccer pinball.

Finally, Colby came pushing through the crowd and, with her knee, corralled the ball into the goal. Lily heard the whistle blow and breathed a sigh of relief. The score was tied 2-2 and the Bombers were still alive. But there were only a few minutes left to play.

Before the restart, the girls gathered in a huddle of sweaty excitement.

Vee led off. "Dudes, there are only a few minutes left, and we've got to get another goal." Vee called everyone "dude." She was the only person Lily knew who could work the word into almost any conversation.

The electricity of competition buzzed in the air. The Bomber fans finally felt like their team had a chance. They knew that soccer is a lot like the ocean–good things tend to come in waves. The Wildcat parents were pacing and quiet. Their coach, a tall lady with curly red hair, had a very worried look on her face.

The Wildcat striker, a firecracker of a player, kicked off and Vee gave chase. Lily watched as Vee forced the forward to pass the ball behind her, keeping the pressure on. Avery moved to help Vee while Lily stuck close to the Wildcat striker, who was facing a losing battle to get the ball up field.

"I'm open," the girl called.

The ball went rolling through the center of the field.

Lily pounced, collecting the pass easily and letting her momentum carry her forward. She touched the ball past one player and kept moving, always looking to make a pass or draw another defender to her. The Wildcats were in disarray. No one stepped up to challenge Lily for the ball, so she kept moving. She thought about a pass, but knew the first rule of a good attacker: If you're open in front of the goal ... SHOOT!

Lily wasn't going to miss this time. She moved to her left, ready to shoot—and felt her feet go out from under her. In a split second she went from about to shoot to a tangle on the ground, fighting to breathe. Someone had hit her from behind. The referee blew his whistle. He pointed to a spot on the ground just outside the box. Lily had been fouled. The Bombers would get a free kick.

Lily barely registered what was happening. She felt as if someone had stuck a vacuum cleaner tube in her mouth and sucked all the air out of her lungs. She couldn't get a breath. Vee rushed over.

"You got the wind knocked out of you," Vee said. "Put your arms over your head and take a deep breath."

Lily nodded and did what she was told. Slowly, her lungs started to refill. She felt awful. Her side ached. Colby came over and whispered to Lily, "Nice work. Way to get the foul. Stay down for a minute more. Groan or something."

Lily still wasn't able to speak and could only give Colby a puzzled look in reply.

"Do you need a break?" the referee asked Lily.

She shook her head. Vee helped her to her feet and waved off their coach.

"I'm fine," she managed to croak. But she wasn't.

"You better take the kick, Vee."

Vee grabbed the ball, lined up for the free kick and waited for the referee's whistle. Lily had lost track of time. She croaked to her coach on the sideline, "How much time?"

Chris held up three skinny fingers.

It was now or never.

Lily heard the beep and watched as Vee's shot curled over the Wildcat's wall, past the keeper and into the back of the net. The Bombers went crazy in celebration—all except for Lily, who was still doubled over.

Chris called for a substitution.

"LJ!" he called. Lily shook her head. She was feeling better, she told herself.

"Let's go, Coach," the referee said. "In or out."

The Wildcats had the ball at midfield and were ready to play. Their coach began to complain that Lily was wasting time. She tried to straighten up.

"Out," Chris said. "Now."

Lily begrudgingly went to the sideline.

"Great playing, LJ," Chris said, "Get some water. Take it easy. You took quite a hit."

Lily collapsed on the ground. Her coach flashed a look of concern. They both knew the Lily James of last season might have thrown a tantrum for having to come off the field–even because of injury. Last year, her emotional behavior had resulted in a two-game suspension. But LJ had vowed this season would be different. She wasn't going to let her temper get the best of her, even if that meant waiting out the last three minutes on the bench.

Plus, the ache in her side was no joke.

The Wildcats came back strong. From the kick-off they moved down the field as one, stringing passes together, working as a team. A tall, thin winger, playing on the outside, took the ball all the way down to the corner flag. Lily struggled to get to her feet. She wanted to yell, "Stop her!" The words wouldn't come. A feeling of dread joined the cramp in her side.

Olivia, the Bombers' clutch defender, read Lily's mind and came in at the last minute. She blocked the cross. Somehow the ball deflected off the winger.

Bombers' ball. Avery, the left midfielder, picked it up for the throw-in.

But Lily watched as Colby sauntered over and took the ball from Avery's hands.

Colby bent down to tie her shoe, black hair flopping over her headband. By now, the Wildcats' coach's face was as red as her hair. Lily worried she was going to explode like some kind of cherry bomb.

"You've got to be kidding me!" the coach bellowed, pointing at Colby.

"Play on!" the referee warned. Colby kept tying her shoe.

"Olivia, go take it," Lily's coach yelled from the sidelines. Olivia sprinted over, grabbed the ball from next to Colby and threw the ball up the line. Lily saw Colby laugh and jog back onto the field.

"One minute left," Lily heard Chris mutter under his breath. "Look alive, defense!"

The Wildcats' center midfielder took control and moved the ball into the Bombers' penalty area. Olivia stepped up to defend. Lily held her breath. Her stomach started to hurt again. When was the referee going to blow the whistle?

As Olivia came in for a tackle, Lily and the rest of the field heard a howl.

"Owww!! My ankle!"

It was Colby. "I stepped in a hole!"

Lily watched, worried, as Colby ripped off her black headband and rolled on the ground.

"Coach!" the referee called Chris onto the field. After a few seconds, Chris helped Colby limp to the sideline. She plopped down a few feet from Lily and gave her a wink.

"Time, Ref!" The coach of the Wildcats was incensed. "Time!" She wanted minutes added onto the game clock.

"Reese," Chris called. He needed a substitute on the field. "Get ready. Quickly."

The referee had his hand on his watch. He was holding the time. Lily groaned. Reese had already taken off her shoes. She thought the game was over.

"This is outrageous!" Lily heard one of the parents yell.

As Reese scrambled to get ready, Colby suddenly rolled over, ran to the sideline, and said, "Coach, I'm okay now!"

"What?" Chris had a tense look on his face. "It's okay, Colby. Just take a rest and get some ice."

"No, really. Look, I'm fine," Colby said, jumping up and down to prove her point.

Chris looked at Reese, who was still trying to jam her foot into her cleat. He sighed, "Okay. Go. Now!"

The spectators booed as Colby retook the field. She was running fine. Clearly, nothing was wrong with her ankle. The referee took out a yellow card.

"What's that for, coach?" Lily asked.

"For wasting time," Chris answered with a shake of his head. The whistle blew. Lily had to admit Colby didn't look very injured. She could hear the whispering from the parents on the other side of the field.

The Wildcats gave one final push, but then time finally did run out. Lily collapsed in a heap when she heard the whistle blow three times. She was thrilled to have vanquished the defending champs, but when Lily saw Colby sprint off the field, questions filled her mind. Was Colby faking? Was she wasting time? And, most importantly, was she right for the Bombers?

Chapter 2.

"Victory!" Lily shouted across the messy hotel room. "Can I have this one?"

"Sure," Colby nodded. "Victory. That's what it's all about, right?"

Lily ripped the word from a colorful sheet of temporary tattoos. Vaulting a pile of dirty soccer clothes, she ran into the small bathroom to get some water while Vee and Olivia sorted through the rest of the tattoo choices.

"How long do I have to hold it?" Lily yelled.

"Fifteen minutes," Colby answered.

"Fifteen minutes?" Lily came out of the bathroom with a wet washcloth on her arm.

"I'm kidding," Colby laughed. "Sucker!"

Lily gave Colby a look.

"Thirty seconds," Colby laughed. "Love the look on your face. Just be sure to lift the paper off slowly so it doesn't tear."

"Look at this one," Olivia said, holding up a flaming

17

soccer ball. "This one is like your shot today, Vee."

Vee smiled. "How long do they stay on again?"

"About a week, depending on how many showers you take and how sweaty you get."

"Whaddya think?" Lily asked, showing off her right arm. Bright green and orange letters covered her skin.

"Oh, love it," Colby said. "We're going to kill 'em tomorrow."

"Can you believe the looks they were giving us at dinner?" Lily asked.

"I didn't know we were all staying in the same hotel," Olivia said. Coming face-to-face with the Baton Ridge Thunder at dinner that night had caught most of the girls by surprise. The Bombers had won their second game easily, and now they faced the Thunder in tomorrow's final.

"The whole tournament is staying here," Colby told them. "It's SOP."

"What's 'sop'?" Vee asked.

"Standard. Operating. Procedure," Colby answered. "Duh."

"The girl in the salad line looked like she wanted you for dinner, Colby," Vee shot back.

"Oh, whatev," Colby said.

"Do you know them?" Vee asked.

"Nah, not really. I might have seen one or two of them at a soccer camp or something over the years. They think they're all that."

"They seemed to know you, dude," Vee said in voice that Lily recognized. Her friend Vee was not digging Colby.

Colby started to respond, but a loud knock on the door interrupted her. All four girls squeaked in surprise.

"Anyone hooomm-eeeeee?" Avery's mother, Mrs. Dwyer, asked, sticking her head into the room.

"Hi-iiiiiiiiiii," the girls answered in unison. Mrs. Dwyer was the Team Mom and their chaperone for the night. She was nice enough, but she had a habit of singing the end of her sentences. Most of the girls couldn't help but do the same in response. Lily, Colby, Olivia and Vee had been assigned the hotel room that connected to the one that Mrs. Dwyer shared with Avery, Sue and Reese. The rest of the Bombers were with their parents in rooms down the hall

"I'm collecting stinky socks. Anyon-eeeeee?" Mrs. Dwyer said. Pinching her nose, she looked with disgust around the room. There were muddy shoes on the beds, clothes pouring out of duffle bags, soccer balls and shin guards strewn on the floor, and one particularly alarming blue puddle on the worn rug in front of the television.

Avery's mom bent down to investigate the stain.

"Melted popsicle," Lily offered. "Blueberry bomb."

Mrs. Dwyer nodded and took a few steps back.

"Well, I can see you're all anxious to have clean uniforms for the big game tomorrow. I'll wash tonight and have them for you by 6:30 tomorrow morning. Okay? Breakfast is at 7 a.m. in the lobby, so be sure to come dressed to go to the game."

The four girls scrambled to gather their ripe belongings. Shreds of grass dribbled from Lily's socks as she handed them over.

"They're still a little wet," Lily said. "Just sweat. I think."

Mrs. Dwyer backed out of the room holding a pile of uniforms.

"Lights out in half an hour. Big game tomorro-ooow!" Mrs. Dwyer said with a coy voice and a sour face.

"Okaaay," the girls mimicked in singsong reply.

Colby closed the door behind her.

"Oh, so glad she's go-ooone," she said, and all four Bombers collapsed in giggles.

"Man, I'm so sore," Olivia said, rubbing her thighs.

"Me too," Lily said. Her legs hurt when she walked, sat, lay down. She plopped down on the bed next to

Vee and admired her new tattoo.

"This is nothing, girls," Colby said. "When you go to ODP, you have, like, three practices a day, and then you hit the gym. Now's that's how you get sore."

"What's ODP?" Olivia asked.

"What's ODP? Are you kidding me? ODP is the Olympic Development Program. You know, where they pick the girls for the national team? Abby Wambach? Alex Morgan? Hello?"

Olivia shrugged her shoulders, embarrassed.

"You guys need to starting learning about REAL soccer if you want to be taken seriously," Colby went on.

Colby had Lily's full attention. Lily wanted to play soccer for the rest of her life. She wanted to score the winning goal in the World Cup. She wanted to win a gold medal at the Olympics. She wanted to make it to the top, and if Colby could help her get there, she was all ears.

"There are going to be some big time scouts at this game tomorrow."

"Scouts for what?" Lily asked.

"College," Colby said solemnly.

"College! We're not even in 8th grade," Lily said.

"Yeah, college. If you aren't on the recruiting radar by 8th grade, you might as well just forget it."

"Come on, Colby." Vee rolled her eyes. "That's ridiculous."

"Is it?" Colby replied. "Mark my words, they'll be there tomorrow and they'll be watching. Which is why we have to win. No matter what."

"No matter what?" Vee muttered, shaking her head. She jumped off the bed, grabbed her toothbrush, and headed for the bathroom. As she pushed open the door, she leaned back and asked, "Hey Colby, how's your ankle?"

She closed the bathroom door behind her without waiting for an answer. Colby ignored the question and motioned for Lily and Olivia to come closer.

"I saw an awesome hot tub out behind the restaurant," she whispered.

"Yeah, so?" Lily asked.

"Let's go check it out. We can loosen up our sore muscles. It'll be perfect."

"It's pitch black out there," Olivia said.

"Exactly. We'll have it all to ourselves."

"Mrs. D is never going to let us go-oo," Lily pointed out.

"Who said we're going to ask? We just have to wait until everyone's asleep," Colby said.

"We will get in so much trouble," Olivia whispered.

"It's only a crime if you get caught," Colby said. "And we're not going to get caught. Trust me, all the big players warm down in a hot tub. It's just what we need."

Chapter 3.

Lily James's heart thwapped in her chest like the churning blades of a helicopter. Somehow, Vee was sleeping soundly in the bed next to her. Lily couldn't imagine how all the jumping and thudding her heart was doing wasn't keeping her friend awake.

Thwap. Thwap. Thud. Thud.

Was Colby really brave enough to sneak out of the hotel room in the middle of the night?

Sure, Lily wanted to soothe her sore muscles like a pro, but she'd never done anything like sneak out before. She'd never even contemplated doing anything like that. Lily saved her most daring exploits and passionate moments for the field. The rest of her life — in school, with family and friends — she hovered right on average.

Thwap. Thud.

This was insanity.

But it was also exciting. Colby was exciting. Lily loved her cool tattoos. She envied Colby's wild hair.

Colby was different, in the best kind of way. Lily gathered a section of her own strawberry blonde hair around her finger as she lay in the bed. For games she always wore a long ponytail, or when she was feeling crazy, two French braids. Next to Colby, Lily's hair was basic and boring. How was anyone going to notice Lily next to someone like Colby?

Vee rolled over. Lily could tell Vee didn't get Colby. Vee wasn't very good at hiding her feelings. Was what Colby had done during the game really that wrong? So she tied her shoe at the end. Big whoop. It's dangerous to play with your shoelaces undone. And she twisted her ankle. Not her fault she stepped in a hole. Lily thought Vee was being a little hard on Colby.

Lily adjusted her pillow and felt a twinge in her side. She hurt all over. Getting the wind knocked out of her was a new, awful experience. Maybe it would be good to relax in a nice warm tub. Lily felt herself calming down, the helicopter circling in to land. Yawning, she pulled the covers over her shoulder and nestled down into the soft sheets. The room was pitch black and quiet.

She was pretty sure Olivia and Colby were already asleep, anyway. Well, it would have been fun, Lily thought. I'm no chicken. I'm brave too. She closed her eyes and started to doze, relieved she didn't have to prove it.

She didn't feel the first poke. The second one made her sit straight up.

"What?" Lily cried out.

"Shhhhhhhhhhh," Colby said. "Here."

Lily's eyes adjusted to the darkness, and she saw Colby and Olivia standing over her bed. Vee shifted slightly next to her. Lily noticed Colby and Olivia both had streaks of black under their eyes.

"Is that eye-black?" she asked.

"Let's move," Olivia ordered.

"Here," Colby said again, shoving something into Lily's hands.

"What's this?"

"T-shirt and shorts. Unless you want to go naked? I don't have a bathing suit. Do you?"

"Oh, right," Lily said. Silently, she changed her clothes. "What time is it?"

"Midnight."

Lily realized she must have fallen asleep.

"Coast is clear, team," Olivia said in a soft staccato voice after poking her head out into the hallway. Lily suddenly imagined her teammate with a fine career in the military.

The three girls crept silently down the hall to the stairs. Their room was on the fourth floor. Quickly, the trio found themselves in the lobby. The receptionist was busy on her iPhone and didn't seem to notice the three barefoot girls scurrying by. They found the door that said PATIO and slipped outside.

It was that easy.

Hot vapor swirled invitingly in the cool night.

Colby went first. Making a face that said the water was scalding hot, she slid slowly into the Jacuzzi.

"Ahhh," she whispered. "Now that's awesome."

Lily and Olivia climbed the steps. Lily paused before getting in. She looked around, but saw only potted plants. She heard muted voices from people in the parking lot behind the hotel.

"Get in," Colby urged.

Olivia went next. Then Lily slipped her foot into the steaming water.

"Ow!" Lily cried, yanking her foot back. She hadn't been in too many hot tubs in her life. "That's hot! Really hot."

"You get used to it," Colby said, lounging in the corner, her arms resting on the sides.

Lily tried again. She could not believe people did this on purpose. Her skin was going to fall off. Olivia, the budding Navy SEAL, didn't seem to be having any problem, Lily noticed.

"Since you're up," Colby said, "How about turning

on the jets? The button is right behind you."

Lily reached back, hit the green button, and saw the pool come to life. Colby and Olivia immediately started trapping bubbles in their t-shirts and shorts. It's now or never, Lily thought. She marched down the first few steps, sucked in her breath, and slowly sank down in the water.

"This. Is. The. Life," Colby said, her head tilted back, black hair sticking up in front like a tuft of grass.

Lily had to agree. "I feel like a celebrity," she said, moving closer to one of the jets. "Plus, I really do think this is helping my muscles."

"I wonder what the Thunder will be like tomorrow? I hear they're really tough," Olivia said.

"Me too," Lily agreed.

"Piece of cake," Colby said. "They have matching bags and stuff. Think that makes them good or something."

Lily turned to the side to massage her sore back. "Man, that really hurt today."

"Yeah, but you got us the free kick; that's all that matters," Colby said.

"How *is* your ankle?" Lily asked. "Did you step in a hole or something?"

Colby rubbed her leg and smiled. "I saw that in the USA-Brazil game. It must have eaten up at least the last three minutes. Just like in the World Cup."

"You mean you didn't really step in a hole?" Olivia asked.

"Look, all the pros do it. Don't you guys watch soccer on TV? When you're ahead, you gotta do what it takes to eat up the last few minutes of a game. I didn't make it up."

Of course Lily watched the World Cups, men's and women's. There *was* a lot of falling down in the final minutes, no question about it. It just had never occurred to her that it was something U13 girls could do.

"But Colby, isn't that cheating?" Lily blurted out.

"Getting hurt isn't cheating, Lily. It's a totally expected part of soccer. Just remember, when you get hurt, even a little, roll on the ground and act like your leg is about to fall off. That way you'll get the free kick or the penalty kick. Everyone does it. You guys need to wake up. If you want to play soccer like the pros, you better do what the pros do. That's how you win."

Lily and Olivia shared a look. Coach Chris had never told them to do anything like that. Lily shifted to massage the other side of her back as she thought. The Bombers lived by the Soccer Sisters Code, the rules they had made up themselves one day when practice was rained out. Falling down and rolling around was definitely not on the list.

But still, Colby seemed so sure of herself. And she knew what she was talking about with SOPs and ODPs.

Lily didn't know what to think. She traced the outline of the tattoo on her arm. VICTORY.

Lily was opening her mouth to tell Colby about the Code when she heard loud footsteps approaching. She looked past the bushes and saw the beam of a strong flashlight bobbing on the path to the hot tub.

"Someone's coming!" Lily said.

"Kill the jets," Colby whispered to Olivia. Olivia jumped out of the Jacuzzi and hit the red button. The hot tub went silent, which only made the footsteps seem louder.

"Hey!" they heard a deep voice yell. "Hot tub closed at ten."

It was hotel security. A tall man with a substantial belly and a serious scowl was approaching. Olivia stood dripping on the patio, eye black smudged across her face.

This was not good.

"What are you doing over there?" he yelled. "This is private property. Don't move."

Olivia's newfound confidence seemed to fly out the window. She looked at Lily. Then at Colby. Lily and Colby's eyes met and they yelled as loudly as they could.

"RUUUUUUUUUUUN!"

Chapter 4.

Olivia took off like a cat with a snake tied to its tail. Lily saw her make a drippy beeline for the rear lobby door. You couldn't miss the squish-squash of her wet clothes and the slap of her feet as she scurried down the path. Lily followed Colby's lead and slunk back into the water as the security guard trudged past.

"Hang on there!" He puffed after Olivia, seeming not to see the other two girls in the hot tub.

"Let's go the other way," Colby said.

Lily and Colby slipped out of the hot tub and ran up the path towards the parking lot, the way the guard had approached. They both peered over their shoulders to see if he was following.

"Oh man," Lily said, "I hope Olivia made it inside."

"No kidding," Colby said. "She'd turn us in in a second."

Lily slowed to a quick, pensive walk. The parking lot was on their left and the hotel was on the right. Everything seemed calm. Now all she could hear was the tiny pitter-patter of water drops trailing from their shorts and hair.

It was eerie.

"How are we going to get back in?" Lily asked.

"I say we go around the front and wait for everything to calm down. We can sneak back into the lobby and up the stairs," Colby answered.

The girls moved past a group of fragrant hedges encircling a light post. As they emerged from the shadows, Colby's eyes widened.

"Oh, lookey what we have here."

It was a golf cart, but a super-duper version. There were doors on the side, windshield wipers, headlights, and even an iPod holder. "Security" was stenciled in bright orange letters across the front.

"Ever drive one of these?" Colby asked.

"I've never even seen one like this," Lily said, running her hand along the fiberglass fender.

"Get in," Colby said, holding one of the doors open.

"Are you nuts?" Lily asked, backing away.

Colby smiled and didn't answer. She climbed into the driver's seat and began fiddling with the buttons on the snazzy dash.

Lily leaned in, looked around, and said, "Colby, you're getting everything all wet. Let's go."

Suddenly, the radio came to life, startling Lily,

"Canvassing rear parking lot. Over."

Lily looked at the back of the hotel. And all the cars.

"Uh, Colby ..." she said.

"Check out these seats!" Colby said.

"Colby, I think this is the rear..."

"I think this is leather!"

"... parking lot!" Lily was frantic. She heard footsteps again. "Colby, let's go!"

Colby didn't budge.

The footsteps got louder.

"Colby, someone's coming!"

Lily looked over the roof of the golf cart and saw the guard running toward them from the front of the hotel. Lily turned to run, but Colby kept fiddling around by the steering wheel.

"Step away from that vehicle!" a voice yelled. Lily grabbed Colby by the arm and tried to pull her out of the golf cart. This was getting out of hand. Lily just wanted to get out of there, grab Colby, find Olivia, and get back in bed where they belonged.

"GET IN!" Colby yelled. Lily's mouth hung open as she saw Colby pull the gearshift. Beep. Beep. Beep. The golf cart began to move in reverse.

"COLBY, NO!" Lily chased the cart as it pulled away.

"He'll catch us on foot, Lily!" Colby shouted.

"Come on!"

Lily shook her head in disbelief, turned, and sprinted back up the path. She dove behind a row of hedges, too scared to do anything but watch.

"Get back here!" the guard yelled. His face was contorted with anger and exertion. Colby took off like Danica Patrick on an Indy 500 straightaway. The out-of-shape guard bent over to catch his breath, and then jogged after her into the parking lot.

He would never have caught them on foot, Lily realized.

A few seconds later, she heard the cart approach. Colby was circling back. A second guard had joined the chase. Uh-oh, this guy is in much better shape, Lily thought. Colby sped closer, zooming past the cars in the lot. The clunky guard tried to block her. Lily saw Colby grin and hook a sharp left toward the Jacuzzi. She careened smoothly away from him and headed straight for the hotel.

But Lily could tell she was going too fast. Colby shrieked as the golf cart clipped the curb and started to spin. Lily held her breath as Colby launched herself from the driver's seat a second before the cart crashed into a sprinkler head. A wet rainbow of water exploded into the night sky.

Colby took off toward the hotel and Lily followed

her, desperate to get back to her room. She could hear the guards swearing loudly, but a quick look over her shoulder told her they were too busy dealing with the broken water pipe and crashed golf cart to care about them.

Lily and Colby snuck back inside the lobby and went quietly up the stairs. On the fourth floor they found a frightened Olivia hiding in the stairwell.

"Lily! Colby! OMG!" Olivia shrieked. "What happened out there?"

Lily started to explain about the wild golf cart chase, but before she could get the words out, Colby started to laugh.

A gut-busting, bent over, double-barrel guffaw.

"Did … did… did …you see the look on that guy's face when he was chasing me?" Colby gasped between breaths. "Man, I thought he was going to split his pants."

She grabbed her sides, tears streaming down her face. Her laughter was contagious. Olivia started to giggle. Despite herself, Lily started to laugh along with them, her fear releasing itself in a fit of laughter.

"I can't believe you took his golf cart!" Lily yelled. "That was unreal!"

"You did what?" Olivia asked.

"Colby took the security guard's cart and they

chased her all over the parking lot!"

Olivia stopped laughing, slack-jawed. "Are you kidding me? Colby, are you crazy?"

"Relax," Colby said.

"Relax?" Olivia said. "When they find us, we're dead meat! We'll be kicked off the team, arrested, suspended, grounded … you name it!"

"They're not going to find us."

Lily felt her thudding helicopter heart taking off again. What if Olivia was right?

"They're not going to find us," Colby repeated. "Because they aren't going to tell anyone what happened."

"What do you mean?" Lily asked.

"Well, for starters, do you think those two guards are going to admit that some girl stole their golf cart and made them look like idiots?"

Lily wasn't convinced. "But what if they do? You crashed the cart into a sprinkler!"

"She what!?" Olivia lay down across three stairs and covered her eyes with her hands. "OMG, OMG, OMG."

Lily nodded.

Colby didn't blink. "There are like two hundred soccer-playing girls staying here. They could never prove it was us."

Olivia looked at Lily. Lily looked at Olivia. Olivia started to giggle again. "She stole a golf cart?"

Lily smiled. "It was pretty crazy. But kind of cool."

Colby stood up and offered Lily a hand. "Cool? It was awesome. Come on, Lily, live a little. And remember," Colby flashed Lily a big smile, "it's only a crime if you get caught."

Chapter 5.

"Hustle over, LJ!" Coach Chris called from in front of the goal. Lily fumbled with her shoelaces and tried to catch up with the rest of her team. The Bombers were already divided into two groups and starting a warm-up game of keep-away in front of the goal.

"I'm here, Coach," Lily said as she joined the closer group. She, Olivia and Colby shared a conspiratorial smile. So far, it seemed Colby was right. No SWAT team had descended on the hotel in search of hot tub-loving soccer players. There was no APB out on a stolen golf cart. Nothing. The sprinkler was off. The hotel was quiet.

"Not there, LJ," Chris said. "You're in this group."

"Oh," said Lily, covering up a yawn. She moved to the second group of players. Vee was in the middle of a circle trying to win the ball from the girls on the outside. It's a good thing Vee's such a sound sleeper, Lily thought, watching her friend zoom tirelessly after the ball. The three Bombers had snuck back into the room, trying to stifle their giggles, dry off and slip back into bed without waking Vee or Avery's mother in the next room over.

Lily reacted a little too late to Avery's pass. As she moved for the ball, Vee popped in between them and stole it.

"You're in the middle, LJ," Vee said.

Lily moved to the inside of the circle, like she'd done countless times before. Usually she could intercept a pass on the second or third try. Today the girls' passes were really sharp.

Or she was really slow.

"Time out," Lily called. Her shoelace was undone again. Lily bent down and for the first time noticed how crowded the field was. Parents, coaches and several of the other teams in the tournament were getting comfortable on the sidelines.

There was a large red and black sign that read, THE THUNDER IS READY TO RUMBLE. There were even a hot dog stand and ice cream truck set up by the road. Lily had never been in such a large tournament before. The competitions near Brookville, a town just north of New York City, felt much smaller. This really is the big time, she thought to herself.

"Do you need some kind of special invitation today, LJ?" a voice asked.

She looked up to see Coach towering above her. Chris had always resembled a living beanpole to Lily. Tall, skinny, and kind of floppy.

"My shoelaces were untied," she explained.

"Again?"

"Again," Lily answered, trying to tie faster, which only caused the laces to jumble into an impressive knot.

Chris sighed and bent down to help. Lily was certain she heard several of his joints crack on the way down.

"Girls, keep passing," he said to the Bombers. To Lily, he asked, "What's with you today, LJ? You nervous or something?"

"No, not at all," Lily answered. And she wasn't. She had been so busy reliving what was by far the most thrilling night of her life that the game had barely crossed her mind.

"Listen, the Thunder is known for their passing. They're really excellent at controlling the ball and moving it around. So you're gonna have to work hard and be patient to win the ball and feed it up to the offense."

"OK. Got it," Lily said, bopping back into the warm-up. She won the ball after a few tries, but she was huffing and puffing by the time the referee blew his whistle to indicate the game was about to start.

Lily searched out Olivia and Colby, but saw they were taking a water break on the sidelines. Lily took her place on the field and willed herself to focus.

From kick-off, she could tell that Chris wasn't kidding about the Thunder. They had her going in circles. The two tall midfielders, in particular, were incredible. One seemed to have Velcro on her cleats and the other just never missed. They passed the ball better than any team she'd ever faced and Lily had to work constantly to even get a foot on it. Her legs were starting to feel like they were filled with sand. Colby took a few weak shots, but they went wide. Vee hadn't even gotten the ball.

For Lily, soccer was normally the sharpest part of her life. Every minute of a match played out in her mind clear as crystal. Each play burned bright in her internal data bank. The sights, smells and noises of a game formed a rainbow of soccer joy and excitement in her memory.

But today she was in a fog. Lily couldn't get moving. She couldn't anticipate where the ball was going. Time was flying, and she kept waiting for something to change.

But all that changed was the score.

The Thunder went up 1-0 off a corner kick in the first minute of the second half.

"Come on," Vee encouraged the team before the restart. "We've got this. We're the Soccer Sisters."

Colby, Olivia and Lily nodded like zombies.

Lily pushed herself harder. She surged forward and intercepted a pass in midfield. Vee was moving down the line and Lily sent a long looping pass to the corner. Colby and Lily made runs for the goal. But this time they didn't communicate and they both ended up on the far post. Vee's cross landed short, and there was no Bomber in place to track it.

The ball dribbled across the face of the goal as Lily and Colby backpedaled to chase it down. The Thunder defender moved to clear the ball, but miscalculated and hit it wrong. The ball soared straight up into the air.

The tall Thunder sweeper called out, "I got it!" and moved to clear the ball with a header. But her teammates didn't move out of the way. She collided with another girl, leaving the ball bouncing awkwardly in the box.

Vee, the closest Bomber, tried to take the shot, but her half-volley went spinning backwards right towards the face of the midfielder with Velcro cleats. The girl raised her hand reflexively just before the ball smacked her right in the nose.

The field froze. The whistle blew.

Hand-ball in the box. Automatic penalty kick.

This was the Bombers' big chance.

"LJ!" Lily heard Chris call from the sideline, but she was already searching for the ball. Lily always took the penalty kicks.

"You want me to take it?" Colby offered.

"Nah, I got this," Lily said, surprised that Colby had even asked. Then she remembered that Colby didn't know that Lily was the Bombers' Penalty Kick Queen.

The referee cleared the stunned Thunder players from the box, and the goalie took her place in the middle of goal. The ref gathered the ball, handed it to Lily, and said, "Wait for my whistle."

Lily nodded. She rolled the ball in her hands, dusting off some small pieces of gravel. She knew that the goalie was watching her. She knew that she was checking her gloves, and getting ready to guess which way Lily was going to shoot. Lily knew better than to look at the goalie. Even more importantly, she knew to never, ever look at the side you were aiming for.

Instead, Lily envisioned the shot in her head like she had done so many times before. She would go to the lower right corner.

She placed the ball on the penalty spot twelve yards out, careful to keep her eyes down and focused on the ball.

Lily could see just the goalie's feet. She noticed that the girl seemed to be standing a little bit to the right of the middle of the goal.

Was the goalie crowding Lily's shot? Did she know Lily always went right?

Don't look, Lily told herself. Just hit it, like you always do.

But the last second Lily couldn't help herself. She broke her own rule. Her brain was muddled and she stole a glance at the goalie.

Their eyes met.

Lily's eyes darted to the right.

Immediately, she cast her eyes back down to the ground. She saw me looking to that right corner, Lily thought. Do I have to go left now?

No, no. I'll go right, she told herself.

The referee drew the whistle to his mouth and a sharp quick beep filled the expectant air.

Lily stepped forward to take the kick, a few paces to the left of the ball. She'd hit it with her instep, straight into the lower right corner, just like she always did.

She kept her eyes down, but in her peripheral vision she could see the goalie bouncing up and down on her line. She knows I'm going right, Lily thought.

"Play!" she heard the referee yell.

Lily stepped up to take the shot, moving deliberately to keep the ball low and hard. But at the last second she changed her mind, and decided to go to the left corner. The problem was, she was too far to the left of the ball. Her timing was wrong.

Everything was wrong.

Lily moved forward and hit the ball straight down the middle. It landed with a thud in the goalie's gut. She'd saved it.

Lily had missed the penalty kick.

The relieved goalie punted the ball high and Lily moved slowly back up the field, her mental haze returning.

The rest of the game zipped by. Before Lily knew it, the final whistle blew.

The Thunder erupted in celebration as the Bombers walked tiredly back to the bench.

Chris was there to welcome them each with a pat on the back.

"You girls gave it your all out there. I'm very proud of you. You worked hard. Now, hold your heads high and go out and congratulate them on a fine win."

Lily trudged out to shake hands with the other team. She raised her eyes only to be faced with the jubilant smiles of the victorious Thunder. Their coaches and parents were beaming with pride from the sidelines, while the Bomber fans clapped with polite disappointment.

Lily replayed the missed penalty kick. In her mind, images of the kick mixed with images from the previous night. Guilt washed over her. She moved slowly to join her team, her head held low, eyes fixed on the ground.

Suddenly, she just wanted to go home.

Chapter 6.

"Three reds, five blues and one black," Lily told her mother, holding up a hodgepodge of mismatched soccer socks.

"All right, so let's get rid of one blue and one red and the lone black," Toni James suggested.

"Get rid of them?" Lily asked, shocked, gathering up all the socks in her arms.

"If you toss the odd ones, you can make pairs of the others."

"But I need all of them." Lily gave her mother a petulant look.

Her mother sighed and grimaced at the mess on the floor. "LJ, you've got to learn to let go of things. Look at these shorts. They must be five sizes too small! Put them in the donation pile."

"But Mom, I scored my first goal in these!"

"Oh, Lily. If you want my help cleaning your room, you have to give up some of this junk."

Lily stared at her mother in shock. Junk? These

were her prized possessions.

"Mom, this isn't even my room, remember?" As Lily spoke, she saw the look on her mother's face and instantly regretted her words.

"How can I forget when you remind me every hour on the hour?" Toni James responded in a sharp tone.

Lily quieted and went back to sorting socks, reluctantly placing the odd ones in the donation pile. She kept the shorts, though. Why did she have to bring up the room situation? Last fall, she had to move into her brother's bedroom when their grandfather, Pop Pop, came to live with them. Pop Pop was old and needed a room with a bathroom, so Lily reluctantly gave up hers. At first, she was miserable about the change, but she'd come to enjoy her grandfather. Who knew an 80-something-year-old could love *American Idol* as much as she did? Even sharing a room with Billy wasn't as bad as she'd thought it would be. Almost every night they read comic books together and told knock-knock jokes until laughter made their stomachs hurt and their parents started yelling from downstairs.

Lily watched as her mom pulled another pile of random items out from under the bunk beds. The last few months had added worry lines to Toni James's pretty face. Recently, Pop Pop had developed a terrible cough that wouldn't go away. Her parents had had to take him to about a zillion doctors. Mom and dad hadn't really told Lily or Billy much about what was going on, but they knew it wasn't great news.

"What about these?" Toni James held up a pair of princess panties that must have been for a four-year-old. "You win any big tournaments with these on, Cinderella?"

Lily laughed, grabbed the underwear, and threw them in the garbage pile. "See, I can get rid of things!"

"Oh, very good," her mom said. Smiling, she got up from the floor. "Sweetheart, my show starts in an hour. I have to get ready. We're dissecting a Palos Verdes Blue, which is ... "

"The rarest butterfly in the world," Lily dutifully replied.

"Very good. Thought to be extinct for over a decade, you know. That is going to be a big event on Bug TV."

Toni James kissed Lily on the top of her head and left the room. Her new web show, *Butterfly CSI*, was a hit in the bug universe. Toni James was known as Madame Butterfly. At least she was working from home now, Lily thought. It was nice to see her more often.

"You going to watch?" Toni called back over her shoulder.

"Yeah, mom," Lily said. "I'll watch it on the

computer downstairs."

Lily went back to the chaos on the floor but quickly lost interest. She looked around for something else to do.

"I'm so bored," she muttered. "Bored and lonely. I'm so bored and lonely I have to tell myself I'm bored and lonely."

From the first day of school, Lily longed for summer to arrive. Now that it was here, she couldn't wait for it to be over. Vee was in Texas visiting relatives, and Lily's other good friend, Tabitha Gordon, was in an all-day ballet camp in New York City. Since the Memorial Day Tournament, soccer was done, and Lily found the days to be hot, empty and endless.

Her next soccer event was the upcoming July 4th tournament, but that was still two weeks away. Lily flopped down on Billy's bottom bunk and gazed up at her favorite poster of the United States Women's National Soccer Team, plastered above the desk. The USA team was in their white uniforms, arms wrapped around one another, sweaty and happy after another victory.

Lily looked down on her arm and saw the remnants of her tattoo. Victory. Very funny, she thought. Only a hint of the V and part of the T were left. They looked like two oddly shaped birthmarks. Lily scratched at the V and thought about the tournament again. She hadn't touched a soccer ball since she'd returned, and she'd never told Vee about her Colby adventures. She tried not to think about the loss or the missed PK, but she stifled a laugh when she remembered the security guards trying to catch Colby in the parking lot. She really is brave, Lily thought. And she was right: We didn't get caught.

Just then, Lily heard a ping from under a pile of sweatpants. It was her new Droid cell phone. Even though it was a big expense for her family, her mom and dad had finally gotten her one. They said it was a reward for learning to control her emotions better, on and off the field.

Ping! Lily rummaged through the pile, knocking over shirts her mother had folded that morning, sending them flying into the air like popcorn. Vee didn't have a cell phone and Tabitha wasn't allowed to text during her dance camp. Who could it be?

When Lily finally found the little black phone, she didn't recognize the number. The area code was 516.

Where is that? Lily wondered. But, it didn't take her long to figure out who the sender was.

"Been to any good hot tubs lately, girl?"

It had to be Colby.

Lily was excited to get a text, but couldn't imagine

how Colby had gotten her number. She asked her.

"Coach," was the immediate reply. "Invited me to play 7/4. Psyched."

That meant Colby was on the roster for the July 4th tournament in Canada. Well, that'll take care of my boredom, Lily thought.

Suddenly, Lily's phone rang. She nearly dropped it in surprise.

"Hello," she answered.

"It's me, Colby. How's it going?"

"Good," Lily said. "But, actually, really boring."

"Yeah, me too," Colby said. "Nothing going on here, either."

"If you were here, we could go kick around," Lily said.

There was a brief pause, and then Colby spoke.

"Well, I was thinking, maybe I should come to your house for a visit. You live in Brookville, right?"

"Are you serious?" Lily asked.

She was. Colby wasn't doing any camps until later in the summer, so her parents had agreed to drive her into New York City. She could take the bus up to see Lily if Lily's Mom and Dad said it was okay. Colby had lied and told her parents there was soccer practice for the July 4th tournament.

"Call you right back." Lily hung up and ran to find

her mother before she started filming.

"Mom!" she yelled, galloping down the hallway. "Mom!"

"What! What is it?" Toni James answered, instantly worried. "Why are you yelling? Are you hurt?" Lily's mom always thought Lily was hurt.

"No, I'm fine. I need to ask you something."

"Not now, I'm about to go on the air." She was preparing her dissection tools.

"No, I need to ask you something supremely important."

"Later," her mom answered, turning back to her work.

"Mom. Pleeeeease. My friend Colby from soccer wants to come and visit for a few days. Can she, Mom? Please, please, please?"

"LJ, I don't have time for this right now."

"Please just say yes, Mom. She can stay in Billy's room with me. I'll donate clothes. Clean the whole house. Everything. Anything. I promise. I'll be nice to Billy. I'll let Pop Pop watch his shows. Please, just say yes."

Toni James shook her head in resignation.

"I have a lot of work this week, and your grandfather isn't feeling very well. I have to take him back to the pulmonologist. I don't have time to entertain you and your friend. I'm sorry."

"We won't be any trouble, Mom, I promise. Please just say yes."

"Okay," she sighed.

"Okay? That's a yes? She can come?"

"Yes, that's a yes. She can come. But please understand, there's a lot going on and I need you girls to entertain yourselves."

"We will, I promise."

Chapter 7.

Lily James had to cut quite a deal with her nine-year-old brother Billy to convince him to sleep on the couch. She had to clear his dishes for a week, help him finish his endless Lego Death Star, and catch twenty-five fireflies. Plus, she had her usual chores: She had to vacuum the living room, organize her books, pull weeds, and wash windows at Katerina's, her father's restaurant downtown. She was going to be busy, but she knew it was totally worth it to have Colby come and visit.

Lily laughed when her Dad, Liam, saw Colby's hair for the first time and did a doozey of a double take. The red stripe was now bright green and the tips of the short, cropped part were neon yellow. But Colby won him over quickly by being a great eater and complimenting his cooking. Food was the fastest way to Liam James's heart.

Colby even played a few heated games of backgammon with Pop Pop, who was surprisingly crafty. Things did get a little testy when Colby and Pop Pop didn't agree on who should get sent home on *Idol*, but it had been a good visit so far. Lily was relieved Colby didn't want to sneak out of the house or anything. Still, after a few days of hanging around and talking soccer, the girls were restless.

"Mom, can we go to town today?" Lily asked at breakfast.

"That's a great idea," her mom answered. "I have to take Pop Pop to the doctor, anyway."

"Can I come?" Billy asked Lily and Colby. "I want to get the new Asterix comic from Longo's Store. It's the Fall of Rome."

Lily was about to answer yes when Colby came out with a whopper.

"Oh, Billy, we'd love for you to come, but I think some of the Bombers are meeting up in town to work on our community service projects. It'll be so boring for you."

Lily's eyes went wide. There was no meeting and no community service planning that she knew about. But she went along with the story.

"We'll read tonight, Bill, after Colby leaves," Lily said. Her brother's long face was hidden by a shock of ginger hair. "Seriously. Maybe I'll even pick it up for you?"

Billy shrugged.

"Yeah, Billy, let them have some girl time. Girls, I love the idea of community service projects. Was that yours, Colby?" Lily's mom asked.

"Well, not entirely. The whole team wants to give back," Colby lied.

"How wonderful," Toni James said. "So, Lily please keep your snazzy new little phone close and check in with your father when you're in town. We'll be back this afternoon."

"Okay, Mom," Lily answered.

The walk to Brookville was just a few blocks. Lily was excited to show Colby around. Lily thought Brookville was a beautiful little town, full of cute shops and cafés. It had an old-fashioned main street with a park, a soda fountain, Longo's comic store, and, of course, her dad's restaurant, Katerina's. Lily was saving that for lunchtime, when they could have anything off the menu for free!

As they waited to cross the street, a commuter bus barreled past. It pulled over and idled at the bus stop a few feet away.

"I have a great idea," Colby said. Grabbing Lily by the arm, she dragged her to the open bus door.

"This the bus to New York City?" Colby asked

the driver. It was a lady. She raised a tired finger to the electronic sign above her head, which read: MANHATTAN EXPRESS/MIDTOWN.

"Perfect," Colby said, fishing in her pocket. She pulled out a yellow MetroCard. "I'll pay for both of us."

"Colby, what are you doing?" Lily asked in alarm as her friend pulled her onto the bus.

"Oh, my dad got me the card. It's cool."

"No, I mean, where are we going? I thought we were just walking to town?"

"We said we were going to town; we didn't say which town. Come on, it'll be fun," Colby answered, bolting to the back of the bus and finding the entire row empty. The doors shut behind Lily while she was still in the stairwell.

Lily followed Colby and said in a low voice, "Colby, my mom doesn't let me go to New York City, not by myself. She's going to freak."

"She's not even going to know," Colby said, stretching out on the seats. "This is the bus I took to get here. I know where it stops. There's a super cool arcade right there. We'll go, check it out, come back in a few hours, and no one will even know."

Lily looked out the grimy bus window. The scenery was changing quickly as they traveled south from Westchester County. Apartment buildings and industrial shops replaced leafy trees. It was too late for her to get off now. Anyway, she had no idea how to get home. She did know that Manhattan was about half an hour away. If they didn't stay very long and got right back on the bus, they could be home in a few hours, long before Lily's mom returned.

The arcade was right where Colby said it would be. Lily started to relax a little. Using the ten dollar bill she'd brought, she bought eight dollars' worth of tokens and played Space Duel, Dragon's Lair, Moon Patrol, and a long battle of air hockey with Colby. The girls used the last two dollars for an ice cream sandwich and headed back to the bus stop.

Lily's phone began to vibrate in her pocket. She looked at the screen.

MOM CELL.

A taxi blared its horn at a passing fire truck. Lily had to cover her ears to block the siren. She went to answer the call.

"No! Don't." Colby said, and hit the ignore button on the phone. "She'll hear all the sirens and horns and know where we are. Nowhere sounds like this but New York City. Text her."

"My mom is better at bugs than technology. She doesn't text."

"Well, whatever you do, don't answer now."

Lily knew Colby was right, but felt terrible not picking up her mother's call. The phone vibrated again.

"Leave it," Colby warned. "Wait until we get back to Brookville. Even the bus will be too obvious."

The bus to Brookville pulled up as if on cue. Lily sighed and looked at her phone's clock. It was 2 PM. With any luck, they'd be home by three. The phone buzzed again, and Lily could feel her mother's worry vibrating through the little machine. Colby reached over and turned it off.

"We'll be back soon; no one's going to know. We're not going to get caught, Lily."

The ride to Manhattan had taken about 25 minutes, but the journey home was more like two hours. The bus crawled along, stuck in rush hour traffic and slowed down by an accident on the highway. Colby said she would handle everything with Lily's parents, but all Lily cared about was getting home and making sure her mother wasn't a total mess.

They leapt off the bus at close to four and sprinted the distance to the James home. Billy was outside on his skateboard. He gave Lily a puzzled look as she and Colby ran down the street.

"She's home," Lily heard her brother yell. Seconds later, Lily's parents burst through the front door.

"LJ!" Her mother ran down the steps. "Where have you been? I've been calling you for hours. Your father said you didn't come to Katerina's for lunch. I've been worried out of my mind!"

Her mother grabbed Lily into a tight hug. When she pulled back, Lily saw tears in her eyes.

"Mom, we're fine. Really," Lily said weakly.

Colby kicked right into gear. "Oh, Mrs. James, this is all my fault. We went to town, but then we were horsing around behind the school, where we maybe shouldn't have been, and by mistake, I knocked Lily's phone out of her hand and down a gutter. Luckily it didn't fall into any water, but we couldn't reach it. We could hear it ringing too, and Lily was dying to answer it, but it took so long for us to get it out. It's all my fault. I should have been more careful."

"So you guys were at the school this entire time?"

"Yeah, we tried everything to get the phone out. Lily told me how important it was to her. We didn't want to come home without it," Colby lied.

"Why didn't you just use her phone?" Billy asked, pointing at Colby.

"Oh, I forgot to charge it last night. Battery's dead," Colby answered without missing a beat.

Toni James looked at Colby for a long minute, and then turned to Lily. "This true?" she asked her daughter.

Lily hated lying to her mother, but she didn't know where the truth was hiding anymore. She nodded and picked at her cuticle, unable to meet her mother's gaze.

"Did you get my comic book at least?" Billy asked, a telling look on his face.

"Oh. No," Lily said, finally happy to tell the truth. "I totally forgot."

Chapter 8.

"Mom, Billy's not helping," Lily complained, carrying another pile of clothes down the stairs.

"Oh, he's too involved with that comic book you got him last night. That was nice of you," Toni James said. Lily glanced at her brother, who was curled up on the living room couch. Lily had gone with her father to get the *Asterix* comic book for Billy after dropping Colby off at the bus stop, and Billy hadn't put it down since.

"You and I can handle this." Lily's mom gave her a warm smile.

"Where should I put these?" Lily asked, looking around the cramped, makeshift bedroom.

"I don't know. I'm still not sure how to make this work," Lily's mom said, a trace of frustration tingeing her voice.

Lily and her mother had been trying all morning to fix up the small den off the living room for Pop Pop. The room was tiny. There was only enough space for a narrow twin bed, an old dresser, a nightstand and a small oxygen tank. Most of the den's original contents were now jammed into a corner of the basement.

"Why are we doing this again?" Lily asked.

"The doctors say going up and down the stairs is too hard on your grandfather's lungs."

"Why?"

"Well, he's not getting enough oxygen, and it makes him short of breath."

Lily stared at the oxygen tank. This was new. It looked a fire extinguisher, except instead of a big black blaster there was a thin, clear tube with two little attachments Pop Pop put in his nose. Her grandfather had started using it several times a day. He didn't like it at all. Mostly, because lack of oxygen had done nothing to cause him any lack of appetite. Pop Pop was still obsessed by food and didn't appreciate little plastic things up his schnoz getting between him and his *antipasti*.

"What's it called again? In his lungs?" Lily asked.

"Emphysema."

"That doesn't sound good," Lily said.

"No, it's not good, but it could have been a lot worse. We didn't know for a while, and that's why he had to see all those doctors." Lily's mom picked up a picture and dusted it off. "Here, this might make it look homier."

Lily peered at the snapshot. The faded photo had been sitting on the dresser in her room for the last few months, but she'd never bothered to look at it. The image was of a young couple: a woman dressed in a winter coat, standing next to a handsome young man wearing a hat. The woman held a small bundle. The Statue of Liberty rose in the background, green and grainy.

"Who is that?" Lily asked.

"That's me," her mom answered.

"Where?"

"I'm the baby. Wrapped up in a blanket. That's your Nanna, and that's Pop Pop. I must have been just a few months old."

"Wow," Lily said, looking closely at the faces in the photo. It was hard to imagine the smiling young couple as her grandparents. She didn't remember her grandmother, who had died when Lily was four years old. Sometimes, Lily forgot that Pop Pop wasn't just her grandfather; he was also her mother's father. Lily would hate to see her own father not getting enough oxygen.

Lily felt an unpleasant knot tying itself up in her chest. Like when Billy sat on her after she hid the remote, but deeper. It made her feel awful inside.

"Look on the bright side, LJ. You can have your room back now," her mom said, and managed a small smile. She left to go get the rest of Pop Pop's clothes.

Lily sat on the bed, holding the picture and feeling like a worm. A lowdown, creepy, slimy worm. She couldn't bring herself to tell her mother about all of Colby's lies. And her own lies, too. Lily wanted to confess, but her mother was so preoccupied with Pop Pop that she couldn't bring herself to make things worse. Her mother probably knew something fishy had gone on, but had let it go because she was too worried about Pop Pop.

Maybe she was lower than a worm, like a … what? Some kind of bug her mother was highly familiar with, Lily thought.

She sat on the bed, looking at the picture. On cue, Pop Pop shuffled in.

"Where's the lunch? Where's your mother?" He asked Lily in his thick Italian accent. Pop Pop had come to the United States from Sicily when he was a teenager. He never liked speaking English, so he spoke Italian to his two daughters and answered Lily and Billy in a jumble of English and Italian.

Lily smiled at the old man. No amount of emphysema was going to keep Pop Pop from food.

"She's upstairs," Lily answered. "I can make you

something to eat."

"*Tu?*" Pop Pop said with a laugh. He clapped his hands in front of himself, and looked at Lily like she couldn't even open a can of soup. "*Ma, sei pazza.*"

"I'm not crazy! I can cook, you know," Lily said. "Dad taught me."

"You can kick," Pop Pop said, although it sounded more like "keekah." Lily's grandfather laughed again at his own joke, but the laugh quickly turned into a cough. A deep hacking cough that made him double over. The sound made Lily feel short of breath. Pop Pop gestured to Lily to help; she jumped up, walked him to the bed, and hooked him up to the oxygen.

The coughing subsided after a few minutes. Lily sat quietly next to Pop Pop. He put his hand over hers.

Toni James came into the den with an armful of clothes. Seeing her father hooked up to his oxygen tank, she asked, "What happened?"

"I told Pop Pop I would make him lunch, and he laughed so hard, he needed help breathing."

Toni James smiled at her dad. "She's not half bad," her mom said. Pop Pop gestured with both hands, fingers to thumbs, which needed no translation. He wasn't buying it.

Lily had dropped the framed photo when she got up to help him. Now she picked it up and put it back on the nightstand, hoping Pop Pop would like seeing it there.

Instead, he became very agitated. Grabbing the picture, his eyes narrowed and he blurted in rapid-fire Italian, "*Ma guarda! Ecco la causa di tutti i miei problemi. Hai visto? 'Na sigaretto in mano anche li.*"

Lily had no idea what was going on. She knew some Italian, but that was too fast.

"What'd he say? What'd he say?" Lily asked, worried that she'd upset him.

"He said … he can see the cause of all his problems," Lily's mother replied.

Pop Pop pointed to the image. "*Guarda bene,*" he said.

Lily knew that meant "look". She peered closely at the image.

"I know, that's mom in the blanket," she said.

"No," her grandfather replied. "Here."

He was pointing at himself in the photo. Finally, Lily saw it. There was a small white cigarette in Pop Pop's hand; a swirl of smoke shadowed the young family. Lily had never seen her grandfather smoke anything in her life.

"I never knew you smoked, Pop Pop." Lily said. "That's gross."

Pop Pop nodded.

"But you stopped, right?" Lily asked.

Her grandfather said something to her mother in Italian. He wanted Lily's mom to translate. But Toni James said, "No, you should tell her this yourself. It's more important that she hear it from you. Especially now."

In slow, careful English, he said, "I knew inside smoking was bad." He poked at his own chest. "I knew it. But I was young. Stupid. I thought I got away with it. But now look at me. *Ricordati.*"

The old man held Lily's face in his gnarled hands. She could hear the wheeze in his voice.

"Remember that, Lily," he said.

Chapter 9.

"Dad, what time are they coming again?" Lily James asked.

"Six o'clock."

"What time is it now?"

"It's uh, 5:59, approximately four minutes since you last asked me the time at 5:54." Liam James looked up from his watch with a mixture of exhaustion and amusement. He was adding charcoal to the grill on the small gray patio next to the family's house.

"What's for dinner again?"

"Oh, it's a surprise from Tomas. We're going to try out some recipes he brought back from his sister in Texas, *frijoles charros* and some *chiles rellenos*."

Lily had no idea what any of that was, but her mouth still watered at the thought. Everything her father made was delicious, and although she could never tell Liam James, everything that Tomas, Vee's father, made was even better. It was *ultra*-delicious. Putting the two of them together was bound to be good.

Lily watched her dad carefully arrange his ingredients on the small table next to the grill, like he was setting up a chessboard. Her stomach growled with hunger — and nervousness. She was anxious to see Vee, who had been away visiting relatives for almost two weeks.

Lily turned back to her brother. After their thumb war had turned too violent, their father had decreed a non-contact waiting game in order. So now they were sitting at the worn wooden picnic table in the backyard playing finger football. The score was tied at 27-27, and Billy was kicking an extra point. If he could flick the little paper triangle through the goal post Lily made by holding her thumbs together, fingers up, he would win the Paper Football Super Bowl. The loser had to set and clear the table, so stakes were high.

"You've got one more minute, Billy. Take your best shot."

"No moving," Billy said, eyeing his sister from across the table. He got eye level with the stadium field (picnic table). It was do or die. He balanced the ball (paper triangle) with his finger and prepared to kick it by flicking it with his forefinger.

"Clock's ticking, Bill. Tick. Tock," Lily said, trying to psych him out.

"Hold on," Billy said, sitting up suddenly. "The ball's falling apart. Time out."

"There are no time outs," Lily said.

"Yes, you get three time outs."

"Okay, thirty seconds. Go." Lily looked around the corner for any sign of Tomas and Vee.

Billy opened the triangle. The ball was simple enough to make, a piece of lined paper folded into a long strip, and then folded up diagonally with the end of the strip tucked into the last fold. Definitely not hi-tech.

Lily thought she heard a car door.

"That them?" she asked her Dad, who had a view of the driveway.

"No, LJ, not yet."

Lily looked back at her brother and saw that he had unfolded the entire ball.

"Bill, your time is up. What are you doing?" she asked. Then she noticed some familiar writing on the paper.

Lily jumped up from her seat.

"The Code!" she yelled, reaching across to grab the paper. Instinctively, Billy pulled back.

"Billy! Give that to me!"

"No, it's my shot!"

"That's the Code! Our honor code! From the Bombers. Where did you get that?"

"LJ, calm down," Liam said immediately.

Lily felt her father's eyes on her. The familiar heat of anger warmed her neck. She inhaled deeply, trying to push the tension away.

She mustered her sweetest tone, "Please, can I have it Billy?"

"Then you forfeit," Billy said, holding the paper behind him.

"Fine, I forfeit. You win," Lily replied.

Billy waved the paper in front of Lily's face, taunting her and keeping it just out of reach. She took another deep breath, but instead of a relaxing exhale, she used the extra oxygen to lunge across the table and scream, "JUST GIVE IT TO ME!"

"LJ!" her father yelled.

A car door slammed in the driveway.

"They're here!" Billy yelled, jumping up from the table and tossing the paper into the air. Lily scrambled to catch it before it hit the ground.

The paper had folds and creases all through it. Lily put it onto the table and tried to straighten it out as best she could. She could hear Vee and Tomas greeting Billy in the driveway. Lily wanted to run to meet her friend, but something kept her glued to the paper. At the top of the page were the words: "SOCCER SISTERS TEAM CODE."

Lily thought back to when her team had written

it. A rainy week in April. A freak storm had blown into town in the middle of practice, and the skies had erupted in a jumble of thunder, hail and wind. The entire team was forced to smoosh themselves into Mrs. Dwyer's Suburban until the other parents could arrive to drive them home.

Chris had suggested they take the time to talk soccer. So the girls decided to create a pact, kind of like club rules for their team. What started out as a bunch of giggling wet girls in a car, turned into a serious debate. They came up with ten rules each Bomber vowed to follow, called it the Code, and nicknamed themselves the Soccer Sisters. All during spring season, they passed the paper around like it was the Declaration of Independence; each girl allowed to hold onto it for just a few days. Lily was the last. At the end of the season, the Soccer Sisters let her keep it. She realized she must have forgotten it in her little brother's room.

Lily recognized the loopy handwriting. It was Olivia's. She had been nominated to write the Code down because she was really good at dotting each "i" with a cute little heart, plus she had a pad of cool blue paper in her backpack.

Soccer Sisters Team Code

1. Team first.
2. Don't be a poor sport or loser.
3. Play with each other and don't take the fun out of it.
4. Never put someone down if they make a mistake.
5. Practice makes perfect.
6. Never give up on the field or on one another.
7. Leave it on the field.
8. Always do the right thing.
9. Bring snacks on assigned days.
10. Beat the boys at recess soccer.

Go Bombers???

Lily scanned the list. She knew the knotted feeling in her stomach wasn't just because her little brother had turned her team's sacred pact into a football triangle. She knew she'd broken the Code.

"Dude!" a voice called. The unmistakable lingo of her best friend.

"Howdy, pardner! How was Texas?" Lily asked with a drawl. She quietly refolded the code and stuffed it into the elastic waistband of her shorts. Vee plopped down on the bench looking tanned and happy.

"Hot," she announced.

"What did you do with your cousins?" Lily asked.

"Well, we hung out. Played a lot of soccer. Rode some horses. Went swimming. Like I said, it was super hot. Oh, and we found this." Vee casually tossed a small plastic bag onto the table.

"What is it?" Lily asked, picking up the bag.

"A scorpion."

Lily dropped the bag with a yelp. "Vee!"

"It's dead, don't worry. I found it under my bed," Vee said. "I brought it back to show your mom. Figured she'd know everything about it."

"That's just wrong," Lily said, trying to imagine sleeping above a deadly scorpion.

"No way! That's awesome!" Billy yelled. "Can I show mom?"

"Sure, that's why I brought it," Vee answered with a grin. Billy snatched up the bag and ran into the house.

"So what did you get up to?" Vee asked. "Did you get your phone finally?"

"Yeah, I got my phone," Lily answered in a flat voice.

"Huh. I thought you'd be happier," Vee said. She knew Lily had been begging for one.

"No, I'm happy." Lily took the folded code into her hand and held it under the table.

"Is that it? Can I see it?" Vee asked.

"Oh, this is just a piece of paper," Lily answered quickly. "But, Vee?"

"That's me. Right here," Vee answered, with a puzzled look.

Lily took a deep breath. "I've got to tell you something."

"Still right here."

"Colby came to stay for a few days."

"Colby?" Vee asked, surprised. "Why did she come here?"

"She's playing in the Robert's Cup. Coach asked her ... Tabitha got a part in some giant ballet in New York, so we don't have enough players. Colby came to visit and practice for a few days."

Vee didn't say anything, but Lily could tell she

wasn't happy. Lily's fingers fiddled with the paper triangle. She took another deep breath.

"Vee?"

"LJ, just spit it out already."

The words were hard to get out, but once the weeks of pent-up lies and secrets started flowing, they spilled from Lily's lips like cars going down a roller coaster.

"Colby came to visit and we took the bus to the city and went to an arcade and then we lied to my mom's face about it. I was supposed to get Billy a comic book, but I lied to him, too. And remember the last game of the tournament? Me, Olivia, and Colby snuck out and went to the hot tub which was awesome, but then it wasn't awesome because the security guards busted us and we ran away and Colby stole a golf cart and crashed it and we didn't get any sleep and I was so tired I played the worst game of my life and we lost and I broke like every single part of the Soccer Sisters Code but we didn't get caught and Colby says if you don't get caught it's not a crime but Pop Pop is sick because he smoked a long time ago and I feel so awful inside; I had to tell you and I know you're going to hate me but ..."

"Dude. Breathe," Vee said, holding up her hand to stop her friend.

Lily took a deep breath. Tears welled up in her

eyes. She stared at Vee, whose mouth had fallen open.

Vee sighed. Lily braced herself.

Finally, Vee spoke, "First of all, I would never hate you."

Lily looked up at her, feeling the knot in her stomach loosen, just a little.

"But," Vee paused, and then launched into her own flood of words, "What the heck is the matter with you? Dude, why don't you just say 'no'? Don't you know how to do that? Did you forget?"

"I don't know," Lily said quietly.

"You are getting pushed around," Vee paused for a minute. "That's just not like you, LJ."

"I guess she is just exciting and I went along with her. Plus, she knows so much about soccer," Lily said.

"Well, she knows a lot about cheap soccer. Colby Wrangle sure doesn't play by our rules," Vee said.

Suddenly the paper triangle felt like an anvil in Lily's hand.

"What am I going to do?" Lily asked.

"What do you mean?"

"I mean, in Canada. When Colby's there. What am I going to do?"

"First of all, you're going to practice saying "no." Second, you're going to remember that this is our team and you're Lily James and you have a mind of your own."

Lily got up and moved to the other side of the table. She hugged Vee tight, relieved to have finally told her everything. They talked about the tournament until dinner was ready, and then stuffed themselves with Tomas' *ultra*-deliciousness. As they ate, Toni James taught them about scorpions. They learned that there are almost 2,000 scorpion species and 30 or 40 have strong enough poison to kill a person. Apparently people in China liked to eat them fried with a mound of ants, but you had to take out the stingers first.

Lily and Vee decided to stick with frijoles.

Chapter 10.

Two weeks later, Lily and Vee were happily squashed in the back of the James's minivan, bookending a duffle bag, soccer balls at their feet, and family luggage looming behind. They were headed to the July 4th Robert's Cup in Montreal, Quebec.

Lily still couldn't believe that her mother, father, brother, grandfather and best friend were taking a road trip together. This was a first. But here they were: Pop Pop snoring like a machine gun in the second row, Billy doing battle on his Nintendo DSI and her parents giggling in the front seat like they were on a date. The minivan hummed along, long stretches of highway floating by like blurry postcard pictures.

Vee and Lily spent most of the drive plotting soccer strategy for the tournament and looking at a picture book about Canada, a gift from Vee's father, who was watching the restaurant so Lily's dad could make the trip. Pop Pop's doctors had given the green light, as long as he didn't walk too far, so there was also a wheelchair strapped to the roof. After the tournament, they were driving over to see Niagara Falls. Apparently Pop Pop had always wanted to visit the awesome waterfall, and had heard hot dogs were cheaper north of the border.

"Why so quiet?" Vee asked.

"Just thinking," Lily said.

"About?" Vee asked.

"Oh, you know. *Everything*," Lily said.

Vee nodded. She knew she couldn't say anything out loud about "everything," so she lowered her voice and whispered with a smile, "I got your back."

In Canada, the Bombers started off with a bang, playing their first game against a team from New Hampshire called the Fire Crackers. They were duds. The Bombers easily went up 2-0 by halftime; the final score was 4-0. Vee had two goals, and Olivia and Colby scored the other two. Lily didn't score but assisted on the last two goals. It was a breeze.

Lily was doing her best to ignore Colby and focus on soccer. Luckily, the night before the first game Lily and Vee stayed with Lily's family on the road, arriving just in time to play. But tonight Lily, Vee, Olivia and Colby were sharing a room at the hotel where the rest of the team was staying. Lily was nervous, but determined to keep her distance.

During the break between games, Colby tried to sit with Lily and talk about their New York adventure, but Lily and Vee found a small table for two at the burger place. Colby finally cornered Lily during warm-up for the second game.

"Man, you have got to see how awesome our hotel is! We stayed there last night. It has an indoor pool on the top floor, a pool table and a huge TV room. We have to check it out," Colby told Lily.

Lily was tying her shoe and didn't answer.

"Lily, you in?"

"I don't think so," Lily said coolly.

"Why not? It'll be crazy," Colby said, apparently oblivious to Lily's mood.

"Colby, I'm just here to play in the tournament and be with my family. That's all I'm doing this weekend."

Lily grabbed her ball and moved away.

"Hey, wait a minute …" Colby called after her, but Lily kept moving.

The second game was a lot tighter. It was against a tough team from Michigan called the Wolfpack. Neither side had much success scoring, but there were close calls for both teams. During the final minutes of the game, Lily took a pass from Colby by the end line. It was a hard, flat delivery, and a Wolfpack defender lunged to intercept. She got her foot in, and the ball deflected off Lily's shin and out of bounds. The linesperson raised his flag and pointed to the corner.

The referee, a tall woman, had been behind the play and had also missed the deflection off Lily's leg.

Colby didn't wait.

"Corner kick!" she yelled, running over to grab the ball.

A corner kick is a terrific scoring opportunity, and Lily knew it. The Bombers needed a goal badly. All she had to do was let Colby kick it in.

Instead, she turned and said, "Referee, the ball hit my foot before it went out. It's a goal kick. It's their ball."

"Thanks, Number 7," the referee replied, pulling out her pen to write something down on the little pad in her front pocket. Lily hoped she wasn't in trouble.

"Goal kick!" the referee called, blowing her whistle.

"But ref, the linesman said it was corner kick!" Colby cried, running towards the corner flag with the ball.

"Colby, it hit my leg. It's a goal kick," Lily said flatly, turning and jogging up field to get in position.

"Number 6, drop the ball. Next time you open your mouth, it's a yellow," the referee said to Colby.

Colby didn't open her mouth, but she did purposely

throw the ball to the corner of the field. The referee immediately blew her whistle and took a yellow card out of her pocket. She called Colby over and held the card up in the air, writing another note in the little book.

Coach Chris immediately called for a substitution and pulled Colby off the field. Lily watched Colby sulk to the sidelines, glaring at her.

Chris kept Colby on the bench for the rest of the game. In the final minutes, Lily and Vee connected with a give-and-go outside the box. Vee fired one of her trademark screamers into the upper corner.

1-0 Bombers.

But the Wolfpack kept up the pressure and the Bombers buckled down. Chris yelled at them to collapse the defense. They only had to hold on for another minute or so.

In their last attack, a Wolfpack defender made a beautiful run down the line. The girl was incredibly fast, with long blonde hair that reminded Lily of Brandi Chastain, one of her all-time favorite players. Vee tracked the defender down the line and managed to corner her near the sideline. Lily moved in to help just as the ball popped loose and Vee went in for a tackle.

The next few seconds unfolded in slow-motion. Vee lunged forward with her right leg, and managed to poke the ball as she slid on the ground. The Wolfpack defender was taken by surprise, but moved forward, driving the ball forward with her stomach. Vee got up quickly and turned to follow, but suddenly cried out and crumpled to the ground.

Vee Merino was the single toughest player Lily had ever seen. She was brave beyond words. She was strong. Vee never went down.

Vee was down and staying down.

Lily didn't even know where the ball was. She rushed over to her friend. Vee was holding her knee, crying.

"Vee! Vee! What happened?"

"I don't know," Vee managed to say through her tears. "When I turned I felt something happen to my knee."

Lily heard the referee's whistle. In an instant, Chris and Lily's parents were by their side on the ground, tending to Vee.

Parents are not allowed on the field during a game, even for an injury. Lily looked around, confused.

"Mom, Vee's hurt. But you have to wait until the game's over."

"The game is over, honey," her mom answered. "You won. I think you just didn't notice."

Lily looked up and saw that the two teams were

solemnly shaking hands. Vee's injury must have happened in the very last seconds of the game.

Lily didn't care. She was only worried about her friend.

Chapter 11.

"Look on the bright side," Lily said. "At least you got a free ride in Pop Pop's wheel chair."

"Dude," was the only reply from a very depressed Vee.

They were sitting together on a long wooden bench in the medical tent, waiting for someone to bring Vee a pair of crutches. Vee's knee was wrapped in ice and propped up on Lily's leg. Lily was a little numb from sitting in the same position for so long, but she was afraid that moving, even a little, would hurt Vee. Vee was being her brave self, but Lily could tell she was in a lot of pain.

There had been quite a few injuries that day, including one concussion, so it was well into the evening by the time the doctor finally saw Vee. Lily's parents stayed as long as they could, but they finally had to take Pop Pop and Billy back to the hotel for dinner. Coach Chris had arrived a few minutes ago and was outside talking with an important-looking man.

Before he left, the doctor told Vee she would probably need to get a test called an MRI to check her ligaments for damage, but that would have to be back in New York.

The tent flap opened. Lily felt the chill from the night air.

"How you girls doing?" A tall man with a beard and glasses approached Lily and Vee. He carried a pair of metal crutches.

"We're okay," Lily answered. Vee was quiet.

"I'm Mr. Markowitz. I'm the Director of the Roberts Tournament," he said in a very kind voice, sitting down next to Vee and Lily. "We're sure sorry that you hurt your knee today, Ms. Merino. Here are some crutches that you can use. Your coach has the report from the doctor. Looks like it might just be a sprain, but you'll need to get yourself checked by your own doctor in a few days. Do you understand all that?"

"Yes," Vee answered. "Thank you."

"You're welcome. I spoke with your father, and I know your coach has, too. Make sure someone gets that report to your dad."

"I'm sure my parents will take care of that," Lily said. "We're BFFs."

"You're what?"

"We're best friends forever."

"Ah, of course. What's your name?" Mr. Markowitz asked.

"I'm Lily James."

"Nice to meet you, Lily." Mr. Markowitz looked at Lily and Vee with a droll smile. "You girls sure look like you could use a shower and some dinner."

"I could eat ten cheeseburgers," Vee answered.

"Maybe twenty," Lily said.

"How long have you been here?" he asked.

"We have no idea," Lily answered.

"Forever," Vee said at the same time.

"You sat with her the whole time?" Mr. Markowitz asked Lily.

"Of course," Lily said, adjusting Vee's ice pack as it slipped to the side. "BFFs, remember?"

Chapter 12.

Lily and Vee didn't make it back to the hotel until close to 10 p.m. Chris took them through the drive-thru of a burger joint so Vee didn't have to walk around. Vee said her knee was starting to feel a little better, but she still couldn't put any pressure on it. Lily and Vee inhaled about six sliders each, with a milkshake, fries, and another slider. Now they were ready to fall straight into bed.

Lily still had to play in the Championship game at noon the next day, but Vee was out for a while. Chris gave them the key to room 314, said he'd see them in the lobby for breakfast, and told them to try and get some rest.

All Lily wanted to do was take a shower, help Vee get settled, and dive into a nice, clean bed. After two games and sitting for so long in the medical tent, Lily was exhausted.

Lily turned the key quietly and cracked open the door, hoping for sleeping girls and silence. Instead,

Colby and Olivia were watching TV and tossing a soccer ball between the two beds.

"Man, what took you guys so long?" Colby asked.

"What took us so long? How about, 'How's your knee, Vee?'" Lily answered. "We've been sitting in the medical tent."

"It didn't look like much of an injury, that's all."

Vee didn't bother to reply. She just crutched her way to the bathroom and shut the door. Lily heard the shower water start.

"I'm tired. Which is my bed?" she asked Olivia and Colby.

"Oh we've been hanging out in both. Whichever one you want," Olivia said.

Lily picked the bed closest to the bathroom to make it easier for Vee.

"We'll sleep here."

"You guys totally missed out," Colby said, throwing the ball up in the air and catching it. "We were swimming in the pool for, like, hours. It was awesome."

"Sounds great, Colby," Lily said, fishing her pajamas out of her luggage. She didn't want to talk about pools, or hot tubs, or really anything with Colby.

"It was great. We're going back later," Colby said.

Lily didn't respond. *Hurry up, Vee*, she thought.

She just wanted to get into the shower and away from Colby.

"Did you hear me?" Colby asked. "We're going back later."

"I don't care what you do," Lily said.

"What's that supposed to mean?"

"Just what I said," Lily turned her back on Colby and pretended to reorganize the clothes in her bag. It didn't work. Colby came around and stood on the other side of the bed, facing Lily.

"Why did you give up our corner kick today? You made me get a yellow."

"I didn't get you a yellow card. You did that on your own."

"You gave away a corner kick," Colby said. "That was stupid."

"No, I didn't. I just didn't lie about it. The ball hit me and went out. It was a goal kick. I think I know what a goal kick is." Lily just wanted the conversation to be over.

"Oh, whatev," Colby said, grabbing the remote and flopping on the other bed.

Vee emerged from the shower and got right into her bed.

"So, let's go," Colby said quietly to Lily.

"Go where?" Lily moved toward the bathroom.

"To the pool. They have a shower there. I said … let's go."

Lily took a deep breath. She could feel Vee watching her from the bed.

"Colby, no. I'm not going anywhere but to bed. We have a huge game tomorrow, and I want to play my best. So read my lips: I am not leaving this room."

Lily got up and went into the steamy bathroom. As she closed the door, she heard Colby say under her breath, "Wanna bet?"

Chapter 13.

It wasn't the siren that woke Lily. It was the pounding on the door.

"Girls! Get up!" Avery's mother was in motion. "Get up! We have to evacuate!" There was nothing sing-songy about her voice, and it got Lily, Olivia and Vee moving quickly.

Fire alarm sirens blasted through the hallway. Automated recordings in English and French kept repeating, *"The fire alarm has been activated. Do not use the elevators. Use the stairs and gather in the lobby. This is not a test."*

Lily helped Vee grab her crutches and hobble down the hallway. Lights blinked in little boxes on the walls, leading them to the stairs.

"Where's Colby?" Lily asked Olivia. Lily had seen Colby in bed asleep, or what looked like sleep, when she got out of the shower. She wasn't with them now, however.

"I don't know," Olivia answered, holding the door

to the stairs open for Vee. "Maybe she's in the pool? It's on the top floor."

Vee soldiered down the first flight of stairs with her crutches, but nearly fell at the top of the second landing. The crutches were too big for her small frame anyway. For the rest of the trip down the stairs, Lily carried them and Vee hopped on her good leg, using the railing for support. She didn't complain the entire way down, but Lily knew it must have hurt.

When they were nearly at the lobby, Lily heard a familiar, welcoming voice. Her mother, father and Billy were helping Pop Pop down the stairs right behind them. Their room was on the sixth floor.

"Oh, LJ, there you are. What a relief. Your father was about to go make sure you were okay." At the sight of Vee hopping, Toni James's brow crinkled. "Poor Vee. How are you managing?"

"I'm fine, Mrs. J.," Vee answered. "I'm a good hopper."

"You're a good egg, is what you are, Vee," Lily's mom said.

Lily saw that Pop Pop was moving slowly with help from Billy and her father. She stepped up to help.

"Where's his oxygen?" she asked.

"There was no time," her father answered. "The Fire Marshall said we had to go."

"I can go back and get it," Lily said.

"*No. Assaloutamente, no!*" Pop Pop barked.

"Okay, Pop Pop," Lily answered.

They made it to the lobby in a group and joined a mass of bleary-eyed hotel guests, most of whom were wearing matching hotel bathrobes. They looked like some kind of giant sleepover party, except that no one was giggling or braiding hair. Everyone had the same startled yet groggy look of concern and irritation at having been rudely awakened by the blare of a fire alarm bell.

"Is there really a fire, Mom?" Billy asked.

"I'm not sure yet," Toni James answered. "But fire alarms don't usually go off in the middle of the night for no reason. We'll have to wait until they check the hotel. For your grandfather's sake, I hope it isn't too long."

Pop Pop had taken a seat on one of the lobby sofas. Lily, Vee and Olivia huddled together with him.

Lily saw Chris jogging across the lobby.

"Ten, eleven, twelve ..." Chris said. "I'm missing one. I need twelve players."

Chris frantically scanned the lobby. Another group of Bombers was gathered with Avery's mom on a second couch. But Lily knew who was missing.

"Chris, Colby's not here," she said.

"What? Where is she? Didn't she come down with you three?"

Before Lily could say no, Colby came running out of the stairwell, breathing hard.

"Twelve. Phew," Chris said when he saw Colby, relief visible on his face.

"Oh, there's Colby," Lily's mom said. "Honey, what took you so long?"

"Oh, well, I was ..." Colby paused to catch her breath. "After I assisted my teammates to safety, I went back up to help some of the elderly hotel guests on the stairs. I'm so sorry if I caused anyone to worry."

Lily opened her mouth to tell Chris and her mother that Colby was lying again. Colby hadn't helped any of her teammates, and Lily was sure she hadn't been helping any elderly guests either.

"Chris!" Lily called to her coach, but he didn't hear her because at that moment the hotel manager's booming French-accented voice filled the lobby.

"Ladies and gentlemen, please forgive this extraordinary inconvenience. The Fire Marshall has just informed me there is no fire. The hotel is safe. A fire alarm was triggered in the upstairs pool area. We are currently investigating. We apologize for the disruption, but your safety is of the utmost importance. Thank you for your cooperation. You may return to your rooms. Please allow those with small children or the elderly access to the elevators first. We hope you will all join us in the Solarium Dining Hall tomorrow for a complimentary continental breakfast. Again, thank you for your cooperation, and good night."

By the time the hotel manager started to repeat the announcement in French, most of the guests were already on their way back to their rooms. Chris told the Bombers that they should take the stairs. Pop Pop was offered the first elevator car by the hotel manager, and Lily walked with him, holding his arm to support him.

"*Grazie cara,*" he said as they moved slowly toward the elevator bank.

"LJ, you can go on up with your grandfather," Chris called after her.

Colby followed them to the elevator and held the doors open for Lily and her family.

As the elevator continued to fill with guests, Lily and her family moved to the back. The doors were closing when Colby moved forward and whispered to Lily, "Told ya."

Chapter 14.

Lily got back to the room as quickly as she could. She knocked loudly on the door, and Olivia answered.

"Hey LJ," she said. "How's your grandfather?"

"He's fine," Lily answered, pushing past her. "Where's Colby?"

"Looking for me?" a voice said. Colby was perched on her bed, a smug smile on her face.

"You did this," Lily accused, pointing at Colby.

"Wasn't that awesome? Did you see all those old farts hobbling around in matching robes? I nearly peed my pants laughing," Colby said. "Oh, and that French manager guy with the crazy accent? That was the best part."

"Wait a minute," Vee interrupted. "Colby, you pulled the fire alarm?"

Lily nodded. "Of course she did."

"Dude!" Vee said, sitting up in bed. "Are you serious?"

"Oh, come on. It was easy. I saw the box up next to

the lifeguard's chair. Piece of cake. The only problem was it turns off the elevators. I didn't know that, so I had to run all the way down. Man, I'm tired. That was the only bummer."

"Only bummer? Colby! One of those old geezers was my grandfather. You know? Pop Pop? He had to walk down six flights of stairs and didn't even have time to get his oxygen tank."

Colby shrugged. "He seemed okay when I saw him."

"I nearly broke my neck hopping down the stairs," Vee chimed in.

"You're fine too. Wow, you guys are a drag.I'm going to sleep," Colby said.

"You don't even care, do you? You don't even get it," Lily said.

"Not really. And I don't know what you're getting all worked up about, Lily. You're the one who snuck out last time."

"Yeah, I did. And you know what? I played the worst game of my life the next day. I missed a penalty kick. I lost the game for us! Sure, I snuck out, but I shouldn't have, and I know that now. I also shouldn't have let you drag me off to Manhattan."

"Whoa. You guys went to Manhattan? Alone?" Olivia asked.

"Yeah, we took the bus to an arcade. It was great," Colby said.

"It was not great!" Lily yelled. "You lied to my mom's face!"

"I got you out of trouble, so, yeah, you're welcome."

"You're welcome? Colby, you can't just go around lying to people. You can't do that! It's wrong!"

"Remember, it's not a crime ..."

"IT DOESN'T MATTER IF YOU DON'T GET CAUGHT! IT'S STILL WRONG!" Lily yelled, not caring if she woke up the entire hotel.

"Okay, dude," she heard Vee say in a quiet voice. Lily took a deep breath. She counted to ten in her head. She took another deep breath. She felt the heat in her neck recede just a little. Practice does make perfect, she thought.

"I'm not going to let you get away with this, Colby," Lily said firmly.

Colby pulled the covers up to her shoulders. "I'm going to sleep, and you're not doing anything. You never do. You don't have the guts.

"Plus, if you turn me in, I'll tell Chris it was you who made me sneak out, and you who took the golf cart. Oh, and I'm pretty sure your mom and dad would be interested to know about our little New York City adventure."

"I don't care if they find out," Lily said.

Colby sat back up and glared at Lily. "Oh, yes, you do. You turn me in, we lose tomorrow. It's as simple as that. Vee's out. Without you, me and Olivia, we won't have enough players."

Lily saw Olivia nodding in agreement.

"She's right, LJ."

"If you turn me in," Colby continued, "Your precious Bombers will have to forfeit the championship. You care, but I don't. You know why? Because I'm not really one of your stupid Soccer Sisters, anyway."

"No," Lily said, as she headed for the door. "You're not."

Chapter 15.

The next morning, Lily wanted coffee for the first time in her life. She had to settle for the sip of Diet Coke her mom gave her on the way to the field. She didn't remember ever being so exhausted. How was she going to make it through the day, much less the rest of the game?

The score was 2-2 by the middle of the second half. The Bombers were holding their own, but fading fast because of their middle-of-the-night false alarm.They were playing a local Canadian team called the Fury.

"Fury" would have also been an appropriate word for the scene in Lily's parent's hotel room the night before. Lily woke up her mother and father and spilled her guts about everything. She told them about the hot tub, the golf cart, sneaking into the city, and how Colby had admitted to setting off the fire alarm.

Lily's father wanted to ground her for life. Lily was in so much trouble that her brother Billy didn't even bother to gloat. Yet facing her mother was worse.

Lily wished Toni James had yelled at her. That would have been easier. But her mother said nothing when Lily confessed to lying to her face. She just stared at her daughter like she was seeing a stranger. The hurt in her mom's eyes crushed Lily. It was a punishment ten times worse than anything her father could come up with—which was saying something.

Lily shook the images from her head and moved for a throw-in, breaking free of a defender and calling for the ball. She was determined not to fall even one step behind. She would not let her team down again. But scenes from the last incredible night still flashed in her mind constantly, even as she ran up field with the ball at her feet.

"I'm packing right now," Liam James had said. "We're going home this second!"

In the end, it was Pop Pop who rescued Lily.

"*Brava*," he said to the room. Then Pop Pop told her parents that at least Lily had been brave enough to finally stand up for herself. He knew how hard that could be. Plus, he was tired, he wasn't going anywhere, and he still wanted to eat hot dogs at the big waterfall.

Lily made a sharp pass out wide to Avery. Avery brought the ball down to the goal line, but missed the cross; the Fury was awarded a goal kick.

As Lily waited for the Fury player to get the ball, she

looked at her teammates, all ready for action in their uniforms, ponytails or braids on every head, looks of concentration teachers would have been thrilled to see in any classroom on every face.

The Soccer Sisters had voted that morning to play short-handed. Or short-footed, as Mrs. Dwyer put it. Lily's parents decided it wasn't fair to punish the whole team for her mistakes. Olivia's parents basically said the same thing when Chris called them that morning, although Lily knew that Olivia was angry at her for turning them in.

Lily wondered if Colby's parents had arrived to pick her up from the hotel yet. As it turned out, the hotel's video cameras had captured the whole fire alarm escapade after all. Lily was grounded, but Colby was in some real trouble.

Lily looked over to the strong Fury midfielder covering her. The whole Fury team spoke French to one another, but Lily knew her name was Ava. Ava had scored the game's first goal on a free kick, and she was sticking to Lily like glue.

The Fury goal kick was low; Lily trapped it on her thigh, moving forward into the box. As she made a move to her right to try and get a shot off, she was jostled from behind. Lily was right in front of the goal. She stumbled hard and saw the referee put his whistle to his mouth. Lily knew if she threw herself on the ground, she would probably be awarded a penalty kick. She heard Colby's voice in her head.

"*Dive! Get the call!*"

Lily thought of the Code. She put her hand on the ground and caught her balance.

The referee yelled, "Play on!"

The Fury goalie picked up the ball and punted it up field. Lily willed her legs to move back into defense, and they went. For some reason, she was running lighter now. She was moving faster. Soccer was clear to her again.

The field felt soft and familiar under her feet, and the hum of the fans and the coaches tickled her ears and inspired her. The weight of her confusion lifted. For the first time in a long time, Lily's mind felt free and soccer felt beautiful.

Ava got the ball at midfield, and made an attacking run down the middle. Olivia was out of position, so Lily gave chase. Ava had some serious moves. Lily kept close. As she approached the box, Ava went down with a yell. Lily knew she hadn't touched her. She didn't know why she'd fallen.

Yelping, Ava held her ankle and rolled back and forth. Lily stopped immediately and bent down to see if she was okay. The ball rolled out of bounds.

"Are you all right?" Lily asked.

"Yes, I'm okay," Ava said in English with a cute French accent. "I think I stepped in a hole."

Lily heard the referee blow the whistle and call for the coach and trainer. She offered her hand to the girl and Ava got up, brushing herself off. The referee waved the coach and trainer off and said, "Blue ball."

Lily ran over to take it, but it didn't feel like it should be her ball. If Ava hadn't stepped in a hole, it would still be the Fury's ball. Lily looked at Chris and he nodded, understanding what she wanted to do. She threw the ball to a Fury defender instead of one of her teammates.

The girl passed the ball to Ava, who immediately shot. She struck it beautifully. With barely even a spin, the ball knuckled its way past Beth, the Bomber's goalie, and the Fury exploded in celebration. The Bombers played their hearts out in the last few minutes, but the Championship was over.

Fury 3, Bombers 2 was the final score.

"I want to go now, Mom," Lily said, as she was greeted on the sideline with a tight hug.

"Okay, honey," Toni James said. "I'm exhausted just watching you run so much. You played great, Lily. I was proud of you today."

"I'm sorry you came all this way to see me lose,"

Lily said.

Lily's mom bent down so that they were at eye level. "I came all this way to see you shine."

Lily and the Bombers gathered up their bags and balls and headed slowly for the cars. Chris and the other parents ruffled Lily's hair and congratulated her on how well she'd played. Even Mr. Markowitz, the Tournament Director, made a point of finding Lily after the game and reminding her, "Don't leave without your medals."

"Oh, Mom, I don't care about any medals today. I just want to go."

"We'll go right after the little ceremony."

Both teams gathered around a makeshift podium, which was really a table by the parking lot. A box on top was filled with trophies for the winners and silver medals for the runners-up. Lily leaned against her mother, watching Ava and her teammates stare excitedly at the prizes.

Mr. Markowitz stepped to the table and said in his booming voice, "Girls, it's been quite a weekend. We have a few trophies to present, so let's get started."

He nodded to an assistant, who gathered up the medals.

"First, to the Brookville Bombers, for a game well played. We thank you for coming all the way to Canada for this exciting event."

There were polite claps all around as the girls moved forward one by one. The assistant placed thick red ribbons around each player's neck.The girls looked forlornly at their second place medals, until Vee crutched to the front. Parents, players and coaches from both teams whooped and cheered her on.

"Yeah, Vee!" Lily shouted above the rest.

Mr. Markowitz quieted the crowd with his hands.

"Now, to our own Montreal Fury, champions of the 50th Annual Roberts Cup!"

A scream arose from the Fury girls as they piled forward to gather their loot.

"Can we go now?" Lily whispered to her mother. Toni James shook her head.

"It's a pleasure to present our Most Valuable Player award," said Mr. Markowitz. From behind the table, his assistant picked up the tallest trophy Lily had ever seen. Wow, she thought. That's huge.

"This year's recipient led her team with six goals for the tournament, including the game-winning goal today. Miss Ava Dubois!"

Lily clapped as Ava stepped forward. Six goals in one tournament was pretty impressive, Lily thought. She hadn't scored any. Ava beamed as she passed the trophy among her teammates.

"Now, to our final award," the Director said.

"Oh good, then we can go." Lily nudged her mother.

"Shush," Toni James said lightly. Lily's father gave Lily a stern look.

"This last award is the most important we give out. Any girl or boy is eligible, from any age group. It's our Sportsmanship Award, and this year, it goes to a player on one of the U13 teams standing here."

A hush came over all the girls as they smiled and looked at one another. The assistant reached behind the table and struggled, trying to lift something. Finally, after some laughter, she brought out the most impressive-looking trophy Lily had ever seen. It was even bigger than the MVP Award!

The assistant handed the gigantic trophy to Mr. Markowitz, who continued, "Being a star off the field is as big a part of soccer as being a star on the field. Some might say it's an even bigger, more important part. You girls were probably not aware, but in every game the referee takes notes on more than just the score. He or she grades each team on their behavior."

There was a murmur among the crowd of parents and coaches. The players looked at one another. Clearly, no one had known the referees were taking notes on the players.

"One girl was recognized by several referees and

by me. For displaying compassion for her friends and opponents, respect for the rules of the game, sportsmanship, and leadership on and off the field, this year's award goes to Miss Lily James of the Brookville Bombers. Lily, come on up here; this is for you."

Lily's jaw dropped as her Soccer Sisters cheered and pushed her forward. Vee gave her a nudge with her crutch. Her mother kissed her cheek and wiped a tear from her face. Her father leaned forward, beaming.

"You're still grounded," he said, and winked.

Lily laughed, taking the heavy trophy in her hands.

Acknowledgements

Lily Out of Bounds is dedicated to my family. We are spread wide and far, but I feel your support and love with every word I write. I have to give special thanks to my brother-in-law, the ultra-talented and patient photographer Evan Rich, for his original photographs and beautiful cover.

Evan took the picture of the Key Biscayne Soccer Club's Girls U11 Blue. Thanks to every one of them, to their Coach Mathias Carrizo, and Team Parent Rita Ineriano. Thanks also to another Key Rat, Mariana Kellogg, for her great interpretation of the Code, loved the hearts! A timeless thanks to my dear friend Jackie Kellogg, for setting it all up, and for inspiring others as President of Key Biscayne Soccer Club.

The Soccer Sisters Code was so fun to create. Lili Romero-DeSimone and her daughter Mica's team, the Alexandria Fire, took my words and made them their own. Thank you for being so wise, so young, and for reminding me about rule #10.

114

Everyone *at In This Together Media* worked tirelessly to make a girls' soccer series a reality. Thank you to Carey Albertine and Saira Rao for your great ideas and support. Lauren Prial and Anna Vogelsinger were instrumental in getting the series off the ground. Thanks also to Megan Murray and Daniella Zalcman for all the social media and website revamp.

Brandi Chastain and Joan Oloff are an amazing team. Thank you both so much for adding your support to this effort. Brandi, you remain an inspiration and you are right, dreams really do come true.

I am also a coach these days, to the Yonkers United Rush U9 girls' team. Thank you my Roadrunners, for keeping me on the field, and on my toes.

Lily is a fictional character, as is her little brother Billy, but as always, I thank children for letting me use their names and for being so excited to come up with the plots!

My final and most heartfelt thank you goes to *In This Together* co-founder, Stacey Vollman Warwick. Stacey, you are *my* real soccer sister. We've been through it all and I can't wait to see what's next. Thank you for everything.

Together Book Clubs: Questions and Activities

1. Why do you think Lily felt so badly during the Bombers' game the morning after her hot tub adventure with Colby?

2. Why did Lily go along with all of Colby's lies to her parents? What would you have done?

3. Should the Bombers' coach have reprimanded Colby more harshly after her unsportsmanlike actions in the first game? What makes someone a bad sport? A good sport?

4. What do you think is the most important lesson Lily learned from her experiences with Colby?

5. What other rules would you include in the Soccer Sisters' Code?

6. If this novel were a movie, which character would

you want to play?

7. Design your own soccer ball for Lily and the rest of the Soccer Sisters to use in their next tournament.

About Andrea Montalbano

Andrea Montalbano grew up on a soccer field in Miami. She continued to play through college acting as captain for her Harvard University soccer team and eventually being inducted into the Harvard Varsity Club Hall of Fame.

After college, Andrea pursued a career in journalism, attending Columbia University's Graduate School of Journalism. She was an English anchor at Vatican Radio, and then worked as a writer and Supervising Producer for NBC News and NBC's TODAY program.

Now the mother of two young players, Andrea is coaching, writing, and bringing all her loves together in Soccer Sisters, the follow-up series to Breakaway (Penguin, 2010). Andrea lives outside of New York City with her husband Diron, and two children.

Discover other titles by Andrea Montalbano:

Breakaway

Connect with Andrea Montalbano:

www.andreamontalbano.com
www.facebook.com/soccersisters
Twitter: @andreasoccer

About Brandi Chastain

Brandi Chastain, NCAA, World Cup and Olympics icon is best known for her game-winning penalty kick against China in the 1999 FIFA Women's World Cup final. She also played on the team that won the inaugural women's World Cup in 1991 and Olympic gold medals in 1996 and 2004. Chastain will be a commentator for NBC covering the upcoming London 2012 Olympic Games.

Brandi is proud to be the Official Spokesperson of the Soccer Sisters Series — our Official Soccer Sister!!

Connect with Brandi Chastain:

www.reachupworld.com
www.brandisworld.com
https://www.facebook.com/www.reachup
Twitter: @brandichastain

Connect with
In This Together Media:

www.inthistogethermedia.com
https://www.facebook.com/InThisTogetherMedia
Twitter: @intogethermedia

Check out the next book in the Soccer Sisters series coming soon!

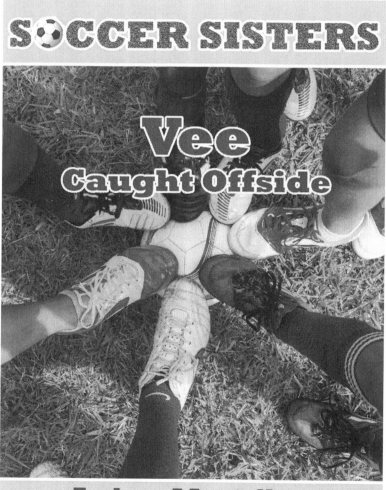

SOCCER SISTERS

Vee
Caught Offside

Andrea Montalbano

17511751R00069

Made in the USA
Lexington, KY
15 September 2012